SOREN

INTERGALACTIC SURROGACY AGENCY

TAYLOR NEPTUNE
JASPER THORNE

APPLICATION

LARA

Being smack dab in the middle of a food shortage when you have a two-year-old to feed is no one's idea of fun. It's even less so when said two-year-old is the messiest eater on planet Earth.

I'm standing in the kitchen watching my sister Janie try to feed Iris, but the little one rejects her advances at every turn, knocking the bottle from her hands and sending it splattering on the floor.

If only she knew how hard we had to work to even get that.

Things have taken a turn for the worse here since the blight swept across the farmlands. Whole farms had to shut down, and getting our hands on food -- especially baby food -- was harder than ever. We'd already had to resort to mixing whole milk with ground rice as a sort of formula-substitute, and even that wouldn't last forever.

The other problem with that gods-blasted blight? It put whole swathes of the population out of work when they needed it most. Namely, me. So here I was, trying to make ends meet on the paltry savings we had left, and trying to do right by my sister and niece.

"We've got to do something," I tell Janie under my breath when she finishes wiping Iris' mouth. "We can't keep on like this."

Janie, usually a bastion of resilience, droops. "I know, but it's not like we're the only ones hurting. Everyone's feeling the pinch right now. No one's coming to save us."

I close my eyes and remember what life used to be like. Before the blight. Before our parents succumbed to illness. Before that slime ball left Janie pregnant and alone as a teen mom.

I glance down at my tablet again, chewing at my lip in thought. I've been wracking my brain over the past few days, reaching out to everyone I can think of and searching for even the most obscure ways to bring in a little extra cash.

"There's something on your mind." Janie doesn't need to ask me. She already knows. Always has.

I don't bother denying it. Just nod.

"What is it?" she asks, her voice tight. She holds Iris on one hip while reaching into the fridge with the other. That's Iris fed -- at least somewhat -- but we still have to feed ourselves. My stomach grumbles as a reminder.

I mull over the words. How could I even bring up something like this?

How could I even consider it? But when I see Iris' sleepy face resting so innocently against Janie's shoulder, I know I have to be strong. For her.

"I've been researching some new job opportunities, and I think I've found something..."

"Oh?" She perks up a bit at that. "Let me go put Iris down for her nap. We can chat on the way."

I follow her out of the kitchen and down the sparse hallway to the room where all three of us sleep. The crib is the nicest piece of furniture in the room. We'd even sold off the bed frame, leaving us with just a mattress on the floor.

Janie said it didn't matter. And it didn't -- to her. She'd sacrificed so much for her daughter. We both had. And I didn't mind sleeping on the floor if it meant Iris could have a crib.

I sit on the edge of the mattress cross-legged while Janie bends over the crib. She lays the little girl down gently in the middle of the bed, then stands back.

For a second, I see tears in the corner of her eyes. They're gone as soon as they arrive, though, and I choose not to say anything about it.

"So... what is it?" Janie's voice is tired. Her face and her posture belie her eighteen years of age. I'm only a year older, and I know I'm not much better.

I swipe open the website on my tablet and hand it to her. I'd wanted to sell this, too -- but Janie wouldn't hear of it. Besides, this was my one remaining connection to the outside world.

I hold my breath as she takes the tablet. Her eyes widen further the more she reads, her mouth dropping into a surprised 'o'. Her brows knit together, and when she reaches the bottom, she looks up at me with concern and confusion.

The seconds tick by in painful silence. Finally, she takes a deep breath and speaks. "You're really considering...this?"

I wince. I knew she wouldn't take it well, but what choice did we have? "I know it sounds crazy, but..."

"Crazy?" Janie's voice cracks into an exhausted laugh. "Yeah, that's one word for it. Being a breeder for an alien? Are you serious?"

"You don't have to say it like that," I mumble.

"Like what?!" She crosses her arms, unconvinced.

"It's not like we're slaves or anything. It's voluntary. And they pay very well -- we wouldn't have to live like this anymore!" I gesture at the empty room. At Iris. "Don't you want that?"

We face off like that for a few seconds more. She opens and closes her mouth wordlessly. "I..."

"Please." My heart weighs heavy at leaving them behind, but I know that the stipend they send will more than cover Janie and Iris' expenses. And not just that -- they'll send food, too. And the way things have gotten, that's almost more valuable than cash.

Janie gives me a long look. "I know better than to try to talk you out of something once you've made up your mind, but are you really sure you want to do this?" Her face darkens. "Iris will grow up without a father because of that asshole. I just...don't want you to go through the same thing. For some wise guy, alien or not, rich or not, to just use you, it's..." Her voice breaks, and I wrap her in my arms.

"I'll be safe," I promise her. "They have all kinds of contracts in place to make sure no one's hurt, and the benefits are out of this world. Plus, it's only for a year. Then I can come back and we can start our new life. Together."

Janie looks up at me, teary-eyed. "I hate that it had to come to this point," she whispers before leaning her head on my shoulder. "But you're right. We're all each other has anymore. All Iris has." With a deep breath, she clears her throat and straightens. "If you're sure, I'm sure. Do what you need to do, Lara. I believe in you."

Her blessing means more to me than she realizes. Little does she know, I was planning to sign up for the program whether she approved or not.

Not because I want to hop in bed with some rich alien just to have his baby. Not because I want to leave my home and my family for a full year. But because Iris is the most important thing in my life right now, and I can't bear to see anything happen to her.

This is my way of protecting her.

She hands me back the tablet, and before I can make any second guesses, I fill out the application.

GENETIC MATCHING

LARA

I'm not sure what I expected, but it wasn't this.

I'm sitting on a cold metal chair in a room with eleven other women. The facility has the bleak, sterile look of a hospital and too-bright fluorescent lights flicker overhead. I fold my hands in my lap and try not to fidget, but then my leg ends up bouncing up and down instead.

The news that I'd been accepted came only two days after submitting the application. We'd both been surprised that it was so soon, but I guess that gave me less time to reconsider.

Now I'm here, sitting in the waiting room, waiting for my name to be called. To pass the time I watch the other girls in the room. Some of them look tired. Others bored. Some of them, I realize with amusement, even look excited.

I think about what their lives must be like. What could have driven them to be here today, same as me. Was it desperation? Curiosity? Pure lust?

I wonder if they're leaving people behind like I will be with Janie and Iris. Or maybe they don't have anyone left, and they're just looking for a way out. The program caters to all types -- that much they made clear on the application.

I'm getting up the courage to say hi to one of the other girls when I hear my name.

"Lara Michaels?"

My head bobs up, and I can't help but gasp when I notice the woman standing there.

My first real, live alien. She stands rather tall for a woman, slightly humanoid but with eyes that are larger than life and skin tinged with a deep, lustrous gold. Stark white hair flows down her back in ethereal waves, and her pointed ears poke out in defined points.

Would the male aliens look like this too?

"Lara Michaels?" The name comes again.

"Oh! Yes, that's me." I stand up a little too quickly, head swimming for a fraction of a second before I right myself. "Sorry, I was..."

"Please follow me." She holds out a hand and her skin glimmers in the light. Fascinating.

I take one last look around the room. There's no backing out now. With a deep breath, I think of Iris -- of her sweet, happy face. Of her laugh.

As long as I keep my eyes on the prize, I can make it through anything.

She leads me down a long, brightly lit corridor. Her strides are long, nearly two of mine, and I rush to keep up.

"Nervous?" She asks as we walk. "I'm Orvox, by the way." Multiple rooms stretch down the hallway, each marked with a number.

"A little," I admit.

She smiles, and even though it looks a bit uncanny on her sharp features, it puts me a little more at ease. "That's all right. I'd be more worried if you weren't. But rest assured, we have taken all the necessary precautions. You'll be in very good hands. Ah -- here we are."

We stop at one marked number three and she opens the door to usher me inside.

Good thing three has always been my lucky number.

THE PHYSICAL PASSES WITHOUT INCIDENT. Well, if you call sitting around in a paper gown while an alien swabs your cheek and pokes and prods you without incident. I know it's part of the process, but that doesn't mean I have to like it.

After I get dressed once more, she tells me to go back to the waiting room while they run some labs. "It'll only be a moment," she promises me, but I know better. I've heard that one before.

My eyes droop. I'm starting to get hungry. I came here first thing in the morning and its already noon. My stomach grumbles; I press a hand to it, muttering silent promises I know I can't keep.

Just a little longer, and I'll be able to eat as much as my belly can hold.

Just a little longer and Iris won't starve.

All I have to do is open my legs for an alien. No pressure.

The swish of the opening doors jolts me awake. It's the same female alien as before, and this time she's holding a tablet not unlike the one I have.

"Ladies, thank you all for being so patient with us today. I'm sure you're all excited and nervous, so I'll get right into it." She taps the tablet and a projection appears in front of her. Okay, not like mine, then.

"I'm happy to announce that the preliminary tests have all come back within satisfactory parameters. The genetic matches are as follows."

Several slides appear on the projection. She flicks through them one by one, eliciting gasps from the gathered girls. I'm not immune. *These* are the guys I'll be staying with?

The first thing I notice is their size. And I don't mean below the belt. Every one of them is built like a brick house with chests bare and muscles bulging. They have the same gold skin, yet somehow it shines even brighter, even more vibrant. They wear their hair long in a variation of braids and shaggy curls. Bright, intelligent eyes seem to bore right through the projection and stare into mine. If I had to compare them to someone on Earth, I would call them giant golden Vikings.

Each man has grizzled and unmistakably masculine features, but instead of feeling intimidated, something curls in my gut when I think of sleeping with one. Maybe it's the pure testosterone oozing off their hardened bodies.

"The ruling class on Aesirheim are warlords," she explains. "They are all highly decorated veterans and have served the planet well. They fought off intruders and secured peace for their peoples, but not without cost. The very enhancements that allowed us to win the war have made it...shall we say, difficult to conceive. That's where each of you come in."

She pulls back the projection until all twelve men are showing at once, rotating around a pock-marked planet.

I glance at the girl next to me. She's staring wide-eyed at the image, her jaw hanging open. I can't blame her -- these creatures are beautiful. Powerful.

But they're also deadly.

"While they are our most elite force of warriors, do not misunderstand. Aesir males cherish their females above all else. You will be treated with nothing but the utmost respect and reverence during your stay. You will have anything your heart desires, so long as you complete your duties."

Open your legs and make a baby. The unsaid words echo in the empty air. Each of us knows what we're getting into, no matter how luxurious she makes it sound.

"Are there any more questions?" She scans the crowd. The girls -- myself included -- are all either too overwhelmed or too nervous to say anything.

"Very well. Please report to the spaceport at 8 am sharp tomorrow morning for your inoculation. Please do not eat or drink for twelve hours beforehand."

She turns on her heel to leave and one of the girls finally pipes up.

"I-inoculation?" Her voice wavers. "What for?"

"It's nothing sinister, I assure you. It will simply help your body adjust to the environment on Aesirheim. It also ensures genetic compatibility with your mate."

It sounds so clinical when she says it like that. Mate.

But I guess that's what I am. Not even that, really. Just a carrier for some alien warlord's baby. I have no illusions that he will love me. He doesn't need to. But as long as Janie and Iris are okay, that doesn't matter.

SPACEPORT

LARA

The spaceport looms large before us, a vast, circular structure with a high dome. The glistening chrome almost blinds me when the morning sunlight hits it just right, and I raise my hand to shield my eyes. Even at this distance I can see the hustle and bustle of activity -- cars coming and going, people crossing to and from the many crosswalks. Funny how things like this still exist when half of us are literally starving to death. But for us, right now? It's my ticket to a better life for all three of us.

It's like an airport, but...different. The whole place feels futuristic and new, like nothing I've ever seen before. Must have been something the aliens put in when they made the deal with Earth.

I crane my neck and try to get a look at the hangars situated behind the dome. I'd never seen a real spaceship before. Now I'm about to fly to an alien planet in one.

"I'm going to miss you," Janie admits, squeezing my hand. "Be safe out there."

"I will," I say, but I can't force away the lump in my throat. "Promise."

When I bring her in for a hug, I hear the sound of her stomach gurgling. We didn't have anything to eat yet this morning, but I guess that means I didn't have any trouble following the no food for twelve hours rule. Janie and Iris on the other hand...

"As soon as I sign the contract and get the shot, they'll release a shipment for you. Just a little longer."

Janie pulls back, eyes wide and watery with tears. "I'll never forget this, Lara. Thank you."

I give her the bravest smile I can, even though my heart is beating out of my chest with nerves. "You and Iris gotta take care of each other, okay? I'll be in touch when I can."

"Deal."

The air hangs heavy with all the things we could have said, but nothing feels good enough in this moment. *It's just a year,* I remind myself. *Just a year.* I know that in the scheme of our whole lives that's not very long, but at the moment it seems like the largest obstacle I've ever faced.

But then Janie hands Iris to me and I feel the soft skin of her hands on my cheek. The wispy tufts of hair that tickle my nose. She looks up at me, oblivious to our situation. I try to remember those gentle, dark eyes. The comforting weight of her small body against mine. I press a kiss to her forehead, and this time the tears really do start flowing.

"Love you, Iris. I'll be back soon. Be good for your mommy, okay?"

Her chubby cheeks flush pink as she nods.

"I'll be back for you both. Don't worry." I kiss her again, then hand her back to her mother. "I'll see you soon."

Janie presses her lips into a thin line, choking back a sob of her own. "Love you, Lara."

"Love you, too."

I turn toward the stream of people and the signs pointing to 'receiving area', but Janie calls out to me one more time.

"Yeah?" I whirl around, thinking she might have forgotten something.

"Hey," she says, mouth turning upward in a sad smile. "If you meet a super hot alien up there, don't forget about us!"

I bark out a laugh at that, and wave one more time. Even in the worst of times, she knew how to lighten the mood. With that thought in mind, I set off toward my new adventure.

* * *

DESPITE THE TRAFFIC outside the spaceport, when I arrive at the designated receiving room, I'm the only one there. I almost think I'm in the wrong place, at first. I step inside and look around, seeing nothing but blank walls and empty chairs.

"Hello?" I call out. I must have read the directions wrong. This couldn't be the place.

"Oh! There you are." A familiar voice startles me and I whirl around. It's the alien lady from yesterday, Orvox. There's only one door, though, and I'm facing it. So how did she even get in here? I shiver. There was so much I still didn't know about these aliens. They had skills and technology we couldn't hope to understand, and here I was putting my very life in their hands.

Last minute jitters fluttered through my gut, but I stood my ground. This was it.

"Looks like you're the first one to arrive today. Are you feeling well?"

A loaded question, that one. "Yeah. I think so."

"I've prepared the final paperwork here, if you're ready." She pulls out a clipboard seemingly from nowhere and hands it over to me.

I take it, scanning down the list. My eyes glaze over with the sheer amount of legalese, but I've already went over all the details online. "This is the last thing you need?" I asked, looking up. "Does that mean...?" I didn't get a chance to finish my question.

"Yes. All the necessary details for your transfer to Aesirheim. As soon as you sign, we'll begin the process."

The process. "You'll release the shipment for my family? They really need it, and..."

Orvox smiles. "Not to worry. It's sitting in wait as we speak. You need only sign and accept the inoculation, and your loved ones will receive the remuneration."

My stomach churns again at the word 'inoculation'. It can't be that bad, right? And if what she told us yesterday was true, it was simply to make sure our bodies could handle the environment on Aesirheim.

Sounded necessary, honestly. I certainly didn't want to suffocate to death on my first day just because I couldn't breathe the air.

"Your signature, please." Orvox brings me back to the present, her voice kindly but firm.

I gulp and look down at the contract one more time. One swipe of a pen and the next year of my life was theirs.

One year of my life in exchange for a better future for all of us. Worth it. I hold my breath and swipe my pen across the page.

INOCULATION

LARA

"This won't hurt a bit," Orvox promises me.

I've heard that one before, too.

I try not to look at the syringe in her hand. Try not to think about what it might do to my body. A strange gold liquid the same color as the alien's skin drips out of it slowly.

I grit my teeth and nod. "Okay." The sooner we could get this over with, the sooner Janie and Iris would get to eat.

Orvox keeps talking while she cleans my shoulder with an alcohol pad and preps the syringe. "I'm going to inject you with a small dose of a universal immune booster. It will help your body acclimate to the environment on Aesirheim. It also contains a pheromone treatment and fertility booster."

Pheromones. Fertility. I wince at the all-too-casual way the words roll off her tongue as if it were the most normal thing in the world. I know what I'm getting myself into, know what it entails, but still, to hear it so plainly like that...

I'm no more than a womb to them. That's all I can ever be.

I swallow hard and close my eyes. "Do it."

* * *

One sharp sting, it's all over. I feel the warm fluid flow through me, and suddenly I feel...better. Like I've been doused in sunshine after being cooped up in a dark room all day. My head clears, and the ache in my muscles fades away.

"That should do it," Orvox says, patting my arm. "Try not to move around too much for ten minutes. Will you be carrying that bag with you?" She points at the small satchel holding some clothes and my tablet. "Aesir warlords pride themselves on providing everything their woman could want, but if you insist..."

"I do." I clutch the bag to my chest. It's the last thing I'll have of Earth once we're up in space. The last reminder of what I left behind.

"Very well." She steps back and gives me a small nod. "I've set a timer for ten minutes. When it chimes, you may go and check in at the hangar. Please take your contract and these medical documents with you." She lays out a thick packet on the table next to me. "They'll be waiting for you downstairs."

With that, Orvox leaves, and I'm alone once more. The silence save for the ticking of the timer doesn't help my racing thoughts. I know I'm confident in my decision, but the fear still remains.

I glance over the contract once more for reassurance. It protects not only them, but also me. If anything happens or I get hurt in any way, they'll call the whole thing off and get me to safety. They'll even uphold their end of the deal and continue sending shipments to my family until the year is up.

The warlords have no incentive to hurt us or make us uncomfortable. To do so would rob them of the *surrogates* they so badly needed.

Unfortunately, that didn't stop the image of some gold-skinned alien monster baring his fangs and taking me right then and there. I shiver at the thought, and I'm not sure if it's entirely fear. I have no idea how I feel about meeting the father of a child I'll never raise.

The timer dings and I sit up, picking up the medical packet and contract. I step out of the spaceport's receiving room with a spring in my step, ready to leave this place behind. No more needles. No more paperwork. Just me and the vast expanse of space. Oh, and a golden space man who wants me to have his babies.

When the elevator drops me off on the lowest level, I marvel at the vastness of the hangar. The floors are sleek and white, filled with alien workers and equipment. A few of the workers turn to me and smile, but none approach. Maybe they know I'm not supposed to talk to them.

A sleek silver ship dominates the hangar, dwarfing the crew around it. A small ramp leads up to a main door, and a tall, broad-shouldered soldier stands guard.

The sheer magnitude of it stuns me, and I feel like I've stepped onto the set of a science fiction film.

Only this time, it's real, and the stakes are higher -- much higher.

I turn to a nearby counter marked 'outbound flights'. It's so tall I can barely see over it, and I'm not even that short of a person. A golden-skinned alien sits behind it, oblivious to my presence.

"Um, hello? I was told to bring these here?" I slide the pack of papers across the desk. The alien takes them without looking up and flips through the pages so fast they blur.

"Good to see you, Miss Michaels." He grins while tapping away at his tablet. "We've been waiting for you. You're the last one to arrive, so go on down to the ramp and we'll get you boarded." He hands me a slip of paper with inscrutable letters on it -- also written in the same glowing golden ink. "This is your ticket. Don't lose it."

"Thank you." I tuck the ticket safely into my pocket and turn to face the ship. I've never even flown on an airplane before, and now I'm about to go to space. Crazy how fast things can change.

The soldier at the foot of the ramp gestures to me from across the hangar. That's my cue. I take a deep breath and walk up to the looming starship. The ramp echoes with every step, and when I reach the guard at the door, he throws his arm up in a salute.

"Um...hi?" Too bad they hadn't given us Alien Etiquette 101. I didn't know whether to salute back, or say something, or...

"Ticket." His voice echoes just like the metal ramp. Deep and sonorous, vibrating in my chest.

"Oh, here." I rummage in my pocket and pull it out, handing it over into his outstretched hand.

He glances at it for a fraction of a second, then gives a stiff nod. "Welcome aboard, Miss Michaels. Please take your seat. We will be lifting off shortly."

The door slides open from bottom to top, and I step inside.

They weren't kidding when they said that this program would attend to our every need. Stepping into the ship felt like stepping into a limousine, with a light scent that reminded me of freshly cut flowers. Luxurious seats made of soft leather line the walls, with a low table in the center set with a variety of exotic fruits and drinks.

The guard walks with me, to ensure that I make it all the way inside. “Thank you," I manage to stutter. My brain -- and stomach -- are still focused on the platter of food before me. He simply smiles and says, "You're welcome."

"Is that..." I point at the tray, feeling a flush rise to my cheeks. "For us?"

He gives a nod. "Of course. Eat as much as you like. You will need to be in your seat for takeoff, however."

My mouth drops open, drool already pooling under my tongue. I barely even register when the door whooshes shut behind me. As much as I want...

I pinch myself, just to make sure I'm not dreaming. I'm not. This is real. I'm really here, and I'm really going to space.

My stomach can't wait any longer. I lunge forward and grab one of the fruits, taking a sloppy bite out of it. It tastes like a caramel apple dipped in dark chocolate, and I moan in delight. The flavors explode on my tongue, like it's been waiting for me to come and claim it.

I take another bite, then another, then another. Before I know it, I've devoured the whole thing. I know I probably look like a fool, tearing into the meal with my hands and groaning with each delicious bite, but I don't care. I'm too busy reveling in the taste of food -- real food.

I do my best to pace myself so I don't get sick. It's not easy, especially when my brain is yelling at me to eat everything in sight, but I slow down and savor every bite.

I can only hope Iris and Janie are eating this well. It feels like a crime to indulge like this when they have so little.

Had, I remind myself. Because of me and what I'm doing here, they'll have food and money to sustain them through the next year. They're safe now.

And hey. If the rest of the year means I get to eat like this, maybe it won't be so bad after all.

A loud hiss from the sides of the craft catches my attention and I look up from my feast like a kid caught in the cookie jar.

"Final flight checks have been completed; all passengers please take your seats and fasten your seatbelts. We will be departing shortly."

My heart flies into my throat at the thought. This was it. I was about to go to *space*. I quickly settle into one of the leather seats next to a floor-to-ceiling window and take one last look at solid ground.

"Take care," I whisper to my sister and niece. "I'll be back soon." My chest swells with emotions -- sadness, trepidation, excitement. Not to mention a little nausea from eating so fast. The air suddenly feels too constricting, pressing in on me like a humid summer day. I know it's just the nerves, but I still gasp a few times, heart racing like a scared rabbit. It's gone as soon as it arrives, and I'm left white-knuckling the armrests for dear life.

Oh, I hope I don't get airsick. Or is it space sick? Is that a thing?

I'm about to find out.

The hull hums as the ship's engines spool up, filling the room with a low thrumming noise. The floor vibrates slightly, doing nothing to quell my anxiety. Fortunately, the hot flash doesn't return.

The rumbling grows louder and with a mighty creak the craft begins to move.

It's surprisingly smooth for such a huge ship, and as the hangar doors open, I see the runway spill out before us.

My heart pounds so hard I can feel it beating in my teeth. I can barely breathe, waiting for the moment we leave the ground -- and Earth -- for the next year. To be able to visit an alien planet is like a dream come true.

The circumstances, on the other hand? No one could have predicted that.

"Prepare for acceleration in 3...2...1..."

The ship launches forward, so fast the seatbelt nearly knocks the wind out of me. The earth flies by in an impossible blur, and with an ear-deafening roar, we're airborne.

I force myself to look out the window. It's the only time I'll get to see something like this, and I want to remember every minute of it. Buildings, streets, cars -- all of it shrinks away as we ascend higher and higher. We reach the clouds, wispy tails of white that fleck dewdrops on the reinforced glass, then climb higher still.

The air filtration and pressurization system kicks in with a low hum, recycling and re-oxygenating the air in the cabin. My ears pop painfully and I wince, doubling over with my hands on my head.

Just get through this, I tell myself through the pain. Ascents and descents are always the hardest part. Once we get into space -- real space -- it'll be smoother. But the roar only continues, driving us up and up and up.

A few perilous minutes later, the very atmosphere seems to 'pop' around us, and just like that, the engines cut to a dull hum and the pain stops. Everything is suddenly...silent. I open my eyes carefully and dare to lift my head.

And there it is. The majesty of space spreads out around us, the Earth a rounded globe growing smaller by the second. Eerie, impossible black floods the viewport, pinpricked by countless stars. It stretches on forever, a sea of shadow and light without any end.

If only Janie could see this.

With that thought in mind, I fish into my bag and pull out my tablet to open the camera app. A photo will never do justice to the sheer magnitude of the universe, but it will have to do.

"Are you okay?"

I blink and look across the cabin. The guard from before stands there, watching me with expressionless eyes.

"I'm...okay." I stammer. That's a lie. I'm not okay.

I'm in space, for crying out loud. I'm going to an alien planet to be knocked up by a warlord. And I'm okay?

"You look a little pale," he observes. "This your first time?"

I swallow my suddenly dry throat. "Yeah. First time on a plane, first time on a spaceship." *First time signing up to be an alien's surrogate...* "It's...a lot."

He doesn't move or react. Just watches me. It's so unlike the friendly banter I shared with Orvox on the way in.

"Ah. It's been a long time since I was..." He stops, frowning over the words. "In your shoes." He tilts his head toward the viewport, eyes glazed over with nostalgia. "I almost forgot what it was like, first time in the black." He crosses his arms and joins me at my side.

By now, the flight is an easy, weightless glide. Space whips by in a dizzying array of black and white. Stars streak past us and leave only lines as their afterimage. I have no idea how fast we're going, but it's faster than anything on Earth goes, that's for sure.

"You will be well on Aesirheim." He says, as if to reassure me. "Do not worry. For now, take in the view that the galaxy has given us." The alien gestures toward the viewport, and I can't help but oblige.

It's one of the most gorgeous sights I've ever seen. I can't help but hope that Aesirheim is everything that I've been promised.

FRESH START

SOREN

The transport's late.

I pace back and forth, clenching and unclenching my fists as I check the port monitor for the fifth time. Aesir ships were always on time when I was the captain. Their pilots must be getting sloppy.

They should have been here by now.

The females that will save our dying people.

It wasn't long ago that our planets entered into an agreement -- they would send compatible females in exchange for our abundance of natural resources. A business transaction, nothing more.

The other Jarls and I put our lives on the line to protect our planet from invaders. We beat back our enemies and conquered all who opposed us, but only just. Because the very edge we needed to win the war had an unintended consequence.

Our best scientists put their heads together and came up with an experimental serum, one that would enhance our fighting capabilities and make us stronger, better, faster.

That should have been the end of it, but we got greedy. After coming back from war, our females began to have miscarriage after miscarriage. It was too widespread to be a coincidence. The health organization launched an investigation, and the results were grim.

The experimental serum -- Alpha, they called it -- altered our DNA. It changed us from the inside out, and without a specific genetic match, carrying a pregnancy to term was no longer guaranteed.

Enter the Intergalactic Surrogacy Program.

It wasn't our first choice, but we were running out of options. Humans were some of the most adaptable species in the whole of the universe. Their genetics made them the perfect universal breeder.

It just so happened that we had something they wanted, and they had something we needed. So the treaty was born.

Now the first shipment of females is late, and I'm starting to wonder if we should have put our trust in Earthlings after all. At long last, a call sign appears on the port monitor. They're coming. They're close.

I let out a breath and straighten my uniform before turning on my heel and heading for the gate. The whole way, my mind buzzes with questions and not enough answers. What would the females be like? Would they be kind, or hostile? And -- the most important question of all -- could they bear our children?

I frown at the thought, running a hand along my braids. If this failed...

No. It wouldn't. It couldn't.

And as for the females? As long as they could carry a child, it didn't much matter what they looked or acted like. I reminded myself for the umpteenth time that it was nothing more than a transaction. Something they want for something we want. Both parties leave happy.

Right?

The sky flushes with red and orange as the ship drops out of the sky, engines powering down as it glides toward the docking gate. Thank the fates, the ship's even in one piece. The heavy doors of the bay slide open to welcome the craft, magnets guiding it to communication and maintenance connectors. A crew rushes out to meet it, and I stand on the balcony looking down. My long fingers grip the metal railing with unusual impatience.

I had seen wars and battles aplenty, and made decisions that directed the very fate of our planet. Yet now, as a cargo ship docked with what might be the most important freight we'd ever seen, I was nervous.

Preposterous.

I came here to observe. To be a silent escort and take the females to their new homes in the breeding center.

But that's when it hits me.

A scent, so unlike anything I've ever smelled before. It hits me like a tidal wave, engulfing my senses and blocking out everything else. A chill runs down my spine and my mouth runs dry.

The ramp extends painfully slowly, echoing down on the floor with a dull clang. The smell gets stronger, and I grip the railing so tightly my knuckles turn white. What is this? What is happening to me?

The surrogacy agency spoke of this, though only briefly. They said that we would know when we'd found a match. I'd asked for clarification, but all they did was smile.

"You'll just know."

And with that delicious scent bearing down on me, I can believe it.

My mate -- my omega -- is inside that ship.

The doors hiss open at long last and I hold my breath. First the pilot, then the officers. They're not what I'm here for. Time slows to a crawl as passengers file into the dock. I scan the crowd, searching for the source of that scent. But the more people that fill the dock, the more the scent fades. Muddles.

I curse under my breath. I want to go down there, to check every one of them until I find her. But I stand my ground. I have a job to do and expectations to uphold, just as she does.

I've stood unflinching in the face of certain destruction before. I've faced down murderous pirates and ravaging hordes. This is no different.

Except instead of my body being in danger, it's my heart.

Wait. There.

In the back of the group, a small figure hesitates. She looks around the bustling landing bay, her eyes wide and her brow creased. She clutches a worn satchel to her chest, as if it will protect her from this strange new world. Then she looks up, and by chance or fate itself, our eyes meet.

It's her. It's only a brief second of contact, but now I know. It's her.

My heart stops. She looks so lost. So small. So afraid. An ache blooms, deep within my heart and spreading outward.

But of course she's afraid -- she's on a foreign planet as a surrogate. As far as Earth goes, they're still babies in the intergalactic sense of things. They have not achieved nearly the heights of technology and space travel that we have.

This must be overwhelming for her.

The need to touch, to hold, to protect grabs me and doesn't let go. I'm debating whether to go down and claim her right now, but the officers are there ushering the humans into a transport. So many smells and feelings surround me in a suffocating array, but there's still her -- so clean, so pure.

She's almost to the transport door, then one of the officers grabs her arm. It's just to help her onto the raised platform --

I'm running by the time he makes contact. My hand clamps around his wrist and I tear him away. "I'll be taking this one myself." My voice quakes with a conviction that surprises even me. My blood rushes with the same hit of adrenaline, the same boost that we felt in the height of battle.

The officer stares at me, speechless. "Sir..."

"Are your aural implants malfunctioning? I said, I'm taking her. The other girls can go to the center. She's coming with me." I draw myself up to my full height, daring him to defy me. "You would defy your Jarl?"

"N-no, sir!" He throws up his hands and backs toward the transport. Good man. "Whatever you say!"

The ache in my chest eases just a little, and then I turn to look at her.

The first emotion that comes across is fear. That much I expected. But there's something else, too. Something that calls out to me like a moth to a flame. That scent, that unnerving, mouth-watering scent that makes me want to ignore everyone and everything else to take her, right on the floor, right now.

That's not even the most incredible part about it. I don't get off to her fear or her feebleness. It's the flush of her cheeks, the fullness of her lips, the ample, round curves of her figure. And if I'm not mistaken, she's feeling this too. The sweet scent of female arousal surrounds her, radiating in waves too thick to ignore.

She's leaning. That's what they called it, when we sat in one of those mindlessly boring information sessions. Alphas -- my brethren and I -- could mate and reproduce with a female that had the opposite mutation. One that they called Omega.

And she was transforming into one before my very eyes.

My mouth drops open only slightly, mirroring her expression of awe. I hadn't planned on meeting her this way. I thought I'd have more time to make a proper introduction. Yet here I was. And here she stood.

I'd almost given up hope on ever finding a match after the Alpha mutation ravaged our bodies. Nobody was compatible. Nobody. That's the whole reason we contracted with the ISA.

Now that I'm here, and she's in front of me, in the flesh, this trade looks like it will be the new beginning I need. Both for myself, and for my people.

And I can't say for sure, but when I look at her dark eyes? Maybe she needs a fresh start as well.

DOCKING

LARA

Back on the ship...

Is it hot in here, or is it just me?

No, seriously. Everything around me prickles and burns, the very air seeming to press inward. It's like the hot flash I had earlier, but more intense. Much more intense.

And this time it isn't going away.

I pluck at the collar of my shirt with one finger, but it's not helping. I tug at the elastic holding my hair up, but it only brings another wave bearing down on me.

What is happening to me?

Burning. Ache. Pressure.

Heat.

That pings something in my addled brain, and I vaguely remember learning about this during orientation. What was it again? I'd been half asleep by that point, but the words echo in my mind, clear as day...

As the serum begins to work its way through your body, you may feel some minor side effects such as hot flashes. This can come along with increased libido and is completely normal, so please do not be alarmed. The effects of the inoculation will help you conceive a healthy baby with your match.

My stomach turns again and I double over, focusing on my breathing. It's normal, I try to remind myself. Totally normal. Totally...

And that's when the fire reaches down there as well. I clench my thighs together even as a rush of wetness seeps between them. This wasn't supposed to happen. This wasn't in the handbook!

I grimace and clench at the armrests as the pulsing, throbbing heat spreads its way down. I knew that the shot would change our bodies, but I didn't realize just how much.

"Please fasten your seatbelts and prepare for landing. We will be docking on Aesirheim in approximately ten minutes."

The pilot's words barely register. The heat takes over and I don't even notice our descent until the doors open and a cool breeze washes over me. I should feel relieved to be back on solid ground, but all I can focus on is the way my body aches.

I take in another gasp of the cool, fresh air. It soothes the burn, but only barely. All right. One step at a time.

Something tugs at my arm and I look up. The guard's there, his normally stoic expression morphed into concern. "We have arrived."

"I know," I pant, reaching down to grab my bag from under the seat. "Just got a little...airsick, is all."

"Hmm." That's not much of a response. He continues to stand there, glowering down at me. I gather myself enough to stand and step out into the aisle. He follows me like a shadow until I reach the main front cabin and it's only then I see the other women that traveled with us.

Having our own private cabins during the trip provided comfort and luxury, but it also meant I didn't get a chance to meet any other surrogates. I can't help but wonder if that's intentional.

Maybe it's a scheme to make sure we don't get too attached.

Two women walk off the ramp in front of me. One's pale and freckled with auburn hair, while the other sports a curly mop of raven-black locks. A third woman stands at the foot of the ramp, talking to one of the guards.

They're all beautiful in their own ways. Unlike me. I can't help but feel like a giant, clumsy oaf next to them. They're impossibly tall and slender. I'm...not.

I make my way down the ramp on shaky legs, scanning the crowds and taking in the new landscape. It's like nothing I've ever seen before -- alien in every way. Large stones, black with golden veins, jut up from the ground like talons.

The ground is a strange combination of rock and moss that leaves a dark blue imprint wherever I step. It's like the ground is one giant mood ring.

I wonder what color "scared out of my wits" would be.

I take another breath and smell kelp and brine. It's the unmistakable smell of an ocean. It reminds me of visiting the beach when I was a little girl, and that thought gives me a moment's peace.

"Come on, this way." A firm voice jolts me out of my thoughts and I watch as they herd the surrogates toward a waiting transport. "We'll be taking you to the resort so that you can get settled."

Resort. I almost snort at the word. Like this is some kind of fun vacation.

I fall into line and move across the hangar. Everywhere I look, there's something more to see. For a split second, I see the glint of gold out of the corner of my eye, but just like that, it's gone.

And the heat? The all-consuming, unquenchable heat? It stays at a manageable level now that I'm off the ship. The fresh air helps keep it at bay, as does so many other things to focus on.

But the moment I see that flash of gold, all bets are off.

It slams back into me at full force, but I will myself to stay on my feet. I just have to make it a little bit further to the shuttle and then I can sit down and hopefully ride this thing out.

Just a little further...just a little...

I'm at the shuttle ramp, grabbing for the handrail when I slip, and one of the officers lunges forward to catch my fall...

Everything happens so fast after that.

A blur of a man barrels through the crowd, pushing people aside in his haste. Onlookers call out and stumble, but he pays them no mind. His sights are set on only one thing: me.

He yanks the officer away from me and he falls to the ground before I can blink. Another second later, and a huge golden alien stands before me. I barely come up to his chest, and when I look up I catch the most arresting eyes I've ever seen in my life.

Something happens, then. Something I can't explain and can't describe. It's like everything fades away into the background, those eyes drawing me in like a black hole that I'm powerless to resist.

And though terror and confusion racks through me, there's something else there. Something stronger.

My body reacts before my brain can catch up. The scent of him surrounds me, fresh rain and dark wood. I draw it in and it mixes with the heat inside me, setting off a chain reaction.

It's like fireworks going off between my legs, turning the discomfort into something much more pleasurable. It's no longer a burn, but a delicious, yearning ache. I want him. More than I've ever wanted anything.

I don't understand it, and it scares me.

But I want him.

He's saying something to the officer, something I can't understand, but I can't tear my eyes away.

The pieces click together at last and I draw in a sharp, shuddering breath. I know who this man is.

I saw his picture back on the slides during orientation. It feels like years ago at this point, but I remember his sharp features all too well.

This is Soren.

This is my alpha.

I didn't expect to meet him so soon, or so suddenly. And the way he just threw that officer to the ground...

This is the man that's supposed to take care of me for the next year? And what's more, this is the man I'm supposed to sleep with? Have babies with?

A war of ideals fights its way out in real time as I watch the interaction between the hulking golden alien and the now-cowering officer. Then out of the corner of my eye I see a familiar face -- it's the alien woman from orientation, Orvox, and she doesn't look happy.

I'm more than happy to step to the side as she confronts the alpha. It's almost comical, her small, lithe frame against his, but she crosses her arms and glares at him in a way not many would dare.

She barks something in a language I can't understand, gesturing at the officer and then at me. I try to make myself small, and consider just getting on the shuttle to get away from all this, but my curiosity -- and that maddening desire -- keeps me rooted to the spot.

The alpha growls, and it reminds me of a predatory beast. Too bad, then, that it sends a jolt of unmistakable pleasure all the way down to my spine, pooling between my legs.

Damn this heat.

They exchange a few more pointed words, and I wish I could understand what they were saying. I know they're talking about me, and I know Orvox isn't happy, but other than that?

When did I become such a hot topic?

I clutch my bag closer to my body and wrap my arms around myself. I don't like being in the spotlight. Never have. But I've put aside my discomfort for the sake of my family many times before, and this time is no different.

Well, except for the fact that I'm literally on an alien planet, and apparently they're already fighting over me.

Some welcome.

After one more menacing growl that does all the wrong things to me, the alpha stands down and Orvox turns to me. Her face turns from intimidating to apologetic in the blink of an eye.

"Sorry about him," she says, switching back to my language. "As you can see, some of the alphas get a bit...over eager. But do not worry, he will not harm you. If he does, he will have to deal with me." She leans in close and presses something into my hand. It's a small circular device with a single button. "If he gives you any more trouble, or you need help for any reason, use this to send out a distress call. We'll be there right away."

I hold it tightly in my hands and tears well up in my eyes for a split second. "Thank you," I whisper. "So do I..." I gesture at the shuttle, and then at the looming alpha. "Do I still need to get on the shuttle, or?"

She frowns and lets out a sigh. "Normally you would, but Soren here insists on escorting you personally. You'll be leaving with him instead."

Soren -- so that's his name. I try to make a mental note, but there's so much new information to digest, there's no doubt it'll be lost in no time. Orvox squeezes my hands one more time, then breaks away and joins the shuttle, waving as the doors slide closed.

A tall, looming presence casts a shadow behind me. I turn to see Soren there, standing only inches away and staring down at me like I stared at the platters of food on board the spaceship.

"Um. Hello. It's nice to--" My sentence finishes with a surprised shriek, because he hoists me into his arms without warning and marches away.

FIRST RIDE

LARA

There's one flaw in this plan. The whole point of taking the shuttle to the intake center was so that we could get adjusted and be fitted with translator devices. Without one, Soren's words are nothing but guttural grumbles.

Soren, and even Orvox, seem to have conveniently forgotten that part.

So here I am, practically flying through the air as Soren carries me god-knows-where, and with each step, my body aches and throbs more and more.

The feel of his strong arms around me and the bulk of his massive chest steady against my own -- it's more than I can handle.

I still don't understand what's happening to me, but there's no escaping it. Soren's warmth and scent fill my body. His muscles work under his smooth, golden skin. Skin that begs to be touched, kissed, worshiped...

I blink, startled at my sudden train of thought. I've never been this horny before. Especially for a man I just met.

But then again, I'd never taken whatever was in that 'omega' shot before, either...

I try to focus on something else, anything else, but the landscape blurs by too fast to catch most of it. In fact, it starts to make me a little woozy, so I bury my face in Soren's warm chest and hope for the best.

"Where are you taking me?" I venture to ask. I don't expect an answer. Unlike Orvox, who is clearly some sort of ambassador, Soren does not speak our tongue. How will we communicate without a translator device? Surely he knows this, right? And he'll provide one for me when we get wherever we're going.

Right?

When we come to a stop, I open my eyes and promptly let out a scream.

The landscape has completely changed -- the bizarre mood-ring sand giving way to lush grass and thick foliage. Standing right in front of me, however, is the biggest beast I've ever seen.

It sports tall, proud antlers like an elk, but has a body more akin to that of a horse. Strange markings trail down its neck and flanks. At the sight of Soren, it turns its head and makes a low, chuffing sound.

He speaks again in his jagged language, and the beast actually responds. Is he talking...to that animal? Then Soren turns his face down to me. It's not so bad up close. In fact, he's actually kind of handsome. In a scary, he'll-probably-kill-me kind of way.

Or fuck me to death.

I shiver at the thought, my body tensing as the reality sets in. Soren is huge, to say the least. Practically twice my size. And if the rest of his body is just as proportional...

I gulp. There's absolutely no way. But my traitorous body doesn't seem to care. It's all I can do to keep my hands to myself, to keep my breathing steady, to make sure I don't spontaneously combust before I can find a place to be alone and take care of this myself...

Before I can try to ask what the ginormous beast is, he lifts me up further and with gentle strength, sits me atop the beast's back.

Oh. Oh *no.*

We're going to *ride* this thing.

I am so, so *screwed.*

THE CREATURE'S fur is soft and warm against my legs, and though it's a bit unsettling to be near such a strange creature, I'm also impressed at its apparent calm.

"What is this?" I ask, knowing I won't get an answer. It makes me feel better to talk, even if it's just to myself. Otherwise I spend too much time in my thoughts, and in my current state...

Yeah, not a good idea.

Soren swings up behind me and settles on the beast, wrapping his thick thighs and strong arms around me. I gasp despite myself, clit throbbing as his warmth engulfs me. He has to know what he's doing to me. I can't be the only one that's feeling this.

I shift my hips ever so slightly, trying to ease some of the pressure. I can't stay still. Not with the way Soren's muscles shift behind me. Not with the smooth rocking back and forth motion of the creature's strides. This is so wrong.

My face flushes with shame and arousal. I knew this would be part of the plan, but actually going through it with a sexy-as-sin alien pressed against me?

Easier said than done.

Soren utters a command and the creature slows its pace as we reach a dirt road. I can see the pointed roofs of cottages in the distance, spread out among towering palm trees. Or at least, whatever this planet's version of palm trees is.

I tense as his hands settle on my thighs. It's only then that I feel the rock-hard rod of his erection pressing into my backside. I suck in a gasp, but it turns into a moan. Before I can stop myself, I'm grinding my ass back into him, desperate for more.

My skin burns where he touches me, and my body trembles, waiting for him to move his hands further up my legs. To part them and give me what I crave.

At this point, I don't care if we have to do it right here, on the back of this giant beast. I need him. If my thunderous pulse is any indication, I won't be able to hold out much longer...

One hand creeps higher, one precious inch at a time. I hold my breath. To my dismay, it ghosts over my mound completely and comes to rest on my abdomen. His hands, I realize, are nearly as wide as my waist. If his hands are that large, then how big is...

His hard-on rubs against me once more, so much thicker than anything I've felt before. Even through his clothes, even from the barest touch, I know he will utterly destroy me. Does the shot they gave us cover that, too?

And why does that sound like heaven right now?

The cottages grow closer, rising toward us in time with my panting breaths. I'm all out of dignity at this point, sweating and clinging to the alpha for dear life while I roll my hips in time with our mount's movements. Soren doesn't protest. He holds me close, large hands wandering, and just when I think I'm about to snap...

He utters a command and the beast stops.

Why did it stop? Why did *he* stop?

I open my eyes, and the facility from the orientation greets me. We've arrived.

COTTAGE #047

SOREN

This female is going to be the end of me.

No, I remind myself. Not just any female. Lara.

The very sound of her name thunders through my blood. Her soft body against mine keeps me in a maddening state of arousal the entire ride back to the center. Each breath she takes comes in a quick, shuddering gasp. And her scent -- Aesir, her scent!

It floods every pore of my being. Short circuits my brain and travels straight to my cock. She squirms against me, helpless to my teasing, unable to do anything but take what I give her.

I've fought in countless battles, stared down death more times than I could count, but having this female -- this *omega* so close to me like this is the hardest battle I've ever fought.

It takes everything I have to stop right here and throw her to the ground, heedless of the rules. I want to give her more. I want to show her everything.

I want to make her mine.

But we had a deal. I cannot claim her. Not yet.

And besides, we still cannot understand one another. Not that it is essential for mating, I suppose, but something about her is...different. I want to know more about her. I want to tell her all the filthy things I'm going to do to her, and I want to hear her screams of pleasure as she comes apart on my cock.

To do that, we need a translator.

A frustrated growl rumbles in the back of my throat. I reacted too rashly back at the spaceport. If I'd been thinking with my brain instead of my cock, I would have requisitioned a translator device before we ever left. Before she ever stepped off the ship.

No matter. That can be fixed. All in good time.

All that matters is this present moment, and right now? She's drenched with sweat and arousal. She's so responsive, so supple to my touch. I want to explore more of her. I want to caress every inch, to show her how an Aesir warlord treats a woman.

And more than that? I want to run off with her. To forget all about the contract and take her north, far beyond the reach of the breeding agency. I want to show her off to my people and fuck her so soundly that there's no doubt who she belongs to. I want to see her belly swell with my child.

Good thing there's a sliver of rational thought left in my mind. As much as the primal part of me doesn't like it, I know I have a duty to fulfill. We both have to stay at the facility so that she can be monitored and kept safe.

Pah. As if any Aesir worth his salt would harm a defenseless female. I will have her in every way she desires, but first we must reach the facility.

Our aki slows, lumbering to a halt as it reaches the edge of the facility. Lara looks up, eyes wide and disoriented. I try to speak to her, to calm her trembling form, but she does not listen. Does not understand.

Not for long.

We approach the guard tower and the Aesir inside gives me a wary glance. I call out to him.

"Where are the translators?" I ask, but it's more of a command.

The guard shifts, throat bobbing.

"Ah, they...the Earthlings are to be brought to the intake center, and they will receive all necessary materials there--"

"That's not what I asked." My voice hardens. I could snap his neck here and now, but I have an omega to look after. She comes first, even before my own self. And right now, she needs a translator.

"Where are the translators?" I ask again, narrowing my eyes and projecting my influence.

Lucky for him, the guard makes the smart choice. He points wordlessly at a storage shed nearby and I nod. "Open it," I bark, knowing that it will be locked.

"S-sir..."

"Now."

The pathetic excuse for a guard rushes to the shed and wrenches it open, returning with the treasured device. As soon as I have it safely in my hands, I turn our aki around. Good thing I looked at her file -- I know which cottage she'll be in.

And if her heavy breathing is any indication? She doesn't want to sit through any more introductory meetings either.

Lara is mine, and the moment we enter that cottage, she will know just how mine she is.

WE PULL UP TO THE COTTAGE -- #047 -- and not a moment too soon. I scan the environment as we approach, looking for any signs of danger. There are none. It's quite a quaint little establishment. Furnished with a lovely garden and a front porch, it screams comfort and luxury. Which is exactly what she signed up for.

Anything less and I'd take her away myself, to show her how she deserves to be treated. But yes. This is adequate. There's a biometric scanner on the door so that no one but us can enter, and as I look around I notice there are no other cottages in the immediate vicinity.

Good. That way no one will hear her screams when I bury my face between her legs.

The aki gives a whinny as we pull up to a stop. They've thought of everything -- even leaving a stable area for our mount to rest, eat, and drink.

It hardly crosses my mind, though. Other, more urgent thoughts force their way in, blocking out all sense of reason. Lara looks like she's about to burst, and I'd be lying if I didn't say the same. I make sure she's steady, then I swing down from the mount and look up at her.

Even from this vantage, she's like nothing I've ever seen. Her pleading eyes catch on to mine and don't let go.

"Soon, my omega." I keep my voice soft, hoping she'll catch the emotion behind my words, if not the meaning. I want this just as badly as she does, but we need to get inside first.

I reach up and gently lift her, marveling at her figure once more. She's so light, so delicate compared to my people. It almost feels wrong to bed someone so fragile, but I can't help myself. Her scent drives me crazy and each touch of her perfect skin sends shockwaves straight to my cock.

She wobbles a little as I set her on the ground and she grabs onto me for support. I place a possessive hand at her back and lead her to the door.

My heart thunders in my chest and blood pumps so loudly I hear it pounding in my ears. The moment we're inside, all bets are off.

Lara looks up at me, pointing at the access panel. She asks a question which I assume must be what it is or what to do with it.

The translator still hangs heavy in my pocket. I know I should give it to her, but that would cost precious minutes. And neither of us can really wait another second.

Screw the translator, I growl to myself. I need her now. She needs *me* now.

I gently take her hand and place it against the access panel. It lights up after scanning her palm. She gasps like it's the most magical thing in the world when the door clicks open to let us inside.

Adorable.

If even that is enough to wow her, she's in for a treat here on Aesirheim.

I take one last look around the cottage to make sure there are no intruders, then lead her inside, the door clicking soundly behind us. I can't wait.

INTRODUCTIONS

LARA

When they said we'd be staying in cottages, I'd expected something small and quaint. I imagined something in the picturesque countryside, high in the cool mountains and perhaps not all that accessible. We were here for one thing and one thing only.

But the place Soren leads me to is more like a luxury mansion, and it is definitely on a main road that his mount has no problem navigating. Where do I begin?

First of all, the scanner outside the cottage noticed my handprint and opened up, as if expecting me and only me. I guess the initial scans back on Earth meant that they had all the biometric information they needed from me. When I step inside, I'm in for yet another shock.

High ceilings and smooth, glassy surfaces greet me, along with long, plush sofas and a hearth that's taller than I am. Lights run in neon strips along the ceiling and walls, and the wooden floor is polished to a mirror sheen.

To my right is a kitchen out of my wildest dreams, already stocked with more food than I've ever seen at one time, even before the blight on Earth. And to my left? A marble staircase leading upward to yet more wonders. Floor-to-ceiling windows showcase the lavish gardens and forests around us, and a panel on the wall near the door contains dozens of switches and controls for everything from the temperature to the windows to the lights and even the scents.

They really thought of everything that I could possibly need.

I can't believe all this is really mine, just because I signed a contract and went on a space ship. I pinch my arm just in case I'm dreaming, but the pinch hurts and I don't wake. This is all too real. Any trepidation I had about the contract fades away in the face of such luxury. How could I *not* be comfortable in lodgings like this?

And the company's not bad either...

I turn to look at the golden-skinned alpha alien behind me who took me away from the group to get me on my own. He watches me intently, his dark eyes seeming to bore into my eyes. I back up a few steps, clutching onto the pristine marble of the kitchen bar.

Soren's gaze never leaves mine as he stalks toward me. Every purpose-filled step sends my blood running hotter and hotter. After that ride with him behind me, I'm incredibly wet between my thighs. Everything leading up to now has me teetering on the brink of the most intense, world-shattering orgasm I've ever had and probably will ever have, but we haven't made it over the peak. Not yet.

I lick my lips, desperate for his mouth to be on mine. And yet...shouldn't some kind of introductions be in order? Do we fuck first and get to know each other second? Is that how this works? I have no idea how surrogacy works even on Earth. It wasn't something that I planned for myself. If things had been different, I never would have signed this contract and been on the point of getting into bed with an alien.

"Lara," I offer, pointing to my chest. Then I point at him, hoping he understands. He took a device from the guard back at the center which I can only hope is a translator. Until it's installed, gestures and pantomime will have to do.

It's actually not as hard as it sounds. Soren wears his heart on his sleeve, which is more than I can say for a lot of men.

I don't have to worry about what he's thinking or planning. It's all too obvious, especially when I see the rock-hard bulge stretching his trousers.

"Soren," he rumbles as he approaches, pointing to his own chest in turn.

"Soren," I breathe. His name tastes like the sweetest honey on my tongue, and I can't wait to say it again and again.

Something tells me I'm going to be doing a lot more than that, though, because he picks up his pace and closes the distance between us in an instant. He doesn't waste another second before claiming my mouth with his own.

PLEASURE

SOREN

Hearing my name on her lips breaks what little resolve I have left. I rush to her, wrapping one hand around the back of her head and the other at her back. My thick fingers tangle through her silky hair. I groan deep in my chest before dipping my head down to kiss her for the first time.

It's everything I thought it would be, and more. The taste of her explodes on my tongue, the little moan of surprise she makes only fueling the fire in my chest.

Are all omegas like this? I wonder deliriously as I devour her mouth. Her arms reach out to wrap around me and she melts into my touch, opening her full lips further to let in my tongue. Aesir, she's sweet.

Like the first snowfall of winter. Like the best, most succulent berry of spring, picked ripe from the vine.

There's no one here to bother us. No one to interrupt this perfect moment.

Tonight, she will be mine.

Lara lets out the softest, sweetest little gasp as I pick her up and carry her toward the stairs. Her eyes have that perfect, glazed over look and her lips, pink and swollen from our kiss, part only slightly. It's all I can do not to kiss her again right there.

Control yourself, I try to admonish my primal thoughts. You don't want to scare her, do you?

I dwell on that thought for a moment. And what if I did? If only to show her just how much I wanted her, just how much I craved her scent?

It's more intoxicating than the strongest liquor, and I can't wait to drown in it. And in return, I'll cover her with my scent and my seed so thoroughly no man will doubt who she belongs to.

I know it's part of a contract, but I can't help the way I feel around her. I had no idea these...omegas could be so addictive. So engineered to light up all the worst parts of me, to bring me to my knees in the most primal, bestial sort of way.

One more thought, a tiny spark of hope flickers in the back of my mind. Eclipsed by everything else for the moment, the tiny voice in my head can't help but wonder:

What if she is more than just an omega?

What if she is my heart-mate?

I press my lips together and banish the thought. No. I would never be so lucky.

Tonight is about her, and her only.

I carry her through the cracked bedroom door and kick it shut behind us. My senses crackle and spark like a bonfire as I carry her to the bed. It's a huge, luxurious four-poster with crisp white sheets and downy pillows. If I had my way, she'd stay here forever.

Lara makes a mewling sound in her throat and digs her nails into my back. She looks up at me, eyes wild and pleading.

"Yes," I say, and the word comes from the heart more than from my lips. "You're safe. I've got you."

She smiles and relaxes into my hold as I spread her out on the bed. It strikes me again just how lucky I've gotten as I behold the beautiful human female sprawled out before me. Are all the omegas like this? Are all *humans* like this?

The price we paid feels like such a pittance when I look down at her quivering bosom. Her flushed cheeks. Her thick, smooth thighs peeking out from the bottom of her dress. I take in the delicate fabric and commit it to memory -- she won't be wearing it for much longer.

"Lara," I murmur her name like a prayer and lean down to plant a soft kiss on her forehead. She reaches up to cradle my face in her soft hands and

I trail down to her lips, claiming them once more. She moans and shifts beneath me, and for the first time I let out a deep, rumbling growl as well.

Fuck.

I pull away from her lips only long enough to leave a trail of kisses along her jawline, over her neck, and down her collarbone. Her breath hitches at every touch. Her soft skin presses against me, hot and needy. And who am I to deny my omega?

I take the strap of her dress between my teeth and drag it down and over her shoulder. Each movement is measured, each breath of my own deep and husky. As much as I want to rut into her and hear her scream my name, she deserves so much more than that. She deserves to know just how much an alpha can provide for her.

And I intend to pass with flying colors.

One smooth, round breast falls free from her dress, then the other. Her nipples stand hard and erect, a dark, dusky color that begs to be worshiped. I brush my thumb over one while my mouth closes around the other, circling the bud with my tongue. She throws her head back onto the pillows and cries out, arching her body further up into mine.

"Beautiful," I breathe. My voice and breath hardens her stiff nipples further and I suck it into my mouth once more, rolling the nub between my lips until she's panting and covered with a fine sheen of sweat.

Every time I touch her like this, her scent only grows stronger. The entire room -- no, the entire building *reeks* of it. Does she even realize what an effect she has on me? Does she know how badly I want to fuck her until sunrise, until my seed fills her womb to bursting with my child?

Her breath quickens.

She's about to.

"S-Soren..." Her voice, soft and pleading, is sweeter than the richest honey. She trembles at my every touch. Gasps at my every word.

If she's so sensitive already, I can only imagine how rapturous our mating will be. I could watch her like this all day, but she -- and I -- need more than that. Much more.

I move away from her breasts, trailing my hand and my lips down her supple curves to meet her hips. Her dress is beautiful, but in the way, so I hook one hand behind her back and lift her up enough to pull the fabric over her head.

And what a sight she is. Laying there, completely naked save for her drenched panties, writhing and panting and all but begging me to fill her.

Going slow like this is torture. Pure, sweet, infinite torture -- but I want to remember every little curve of her body. Every soft sigh and shuddering gasp. And the first time she comes apart around my cock, I want to see her face, hear her cries, and fix it in my mind forever.

I slip my fingers under the thin fabric of her panties and pull them down slowly, encouraging her to help me along. Lara takes the hint and kicks them off so quickly she nearly nails me in the face.

Adorable.

I chuckle and kiss her stomach, her hips, her thighs. Everywhere but where we both need it most. My touches orbit the area, growing closer and closer each time, until I'm inches away from her weeping folds.

They told us that our assigned mates would produce a mating 'slick' to ease the process along, but I had no idea there would be so much -- or that it would be so utterly delicious. Her scent is enough to drive me wild on its own, but with this...

I press my nose to her mound and breathe deeply, filling my lungs with her arousal. My little omega is already so close, just from the way I tease her. It is but the first of many orgasms she will have tonight, if I have anything to say about it.

With that, I part her lower lips with my tongue. I tease her entrance first, licking my way up to her swollen bud. I lick circles around it as she cries out and tenses around me, and when I take it into my mouth and suckle every so gently, she screams out my name, bucking and thrusting and spasming against me.

"Soren!" Her voice cracks with the intensity of her cry. That only makes me want her more. I will take everything she has to give me, and then even more than that.

Her juices drip into my mouth as her body thrashes. I groan as she grips my hair and pulls me closer, deeper into her folds, her body trembling and desperate.

I growl with satisfaction and renew my feast with gusto. If my delectable mate wants me, then she will get every orgasm she deserves.

This is what I wanted. For Lara to give herself over to me with no reservations, no hesitation. To trust me with her pleasure. To do what I say, and to come when I tell her.

I drink it all in and start to thrust my tongue into her, fucking her tight, wet cunt with every ounce of strength I possess.

Mm, I could get used to this.

The taste of her fills my head and drives me wild, spurring me on to fuck her harder. I have no idea how long I spend making her cum like this, but she goes through at least three orgasms before she falls limp and wet on the bed. When I look up from her parted thighs, face smeared with her cum, she's panting hard. Her eyes are glassy and distant, as if she's lost in ecstasy. Or already in another world entirely.

"Soren..." She breathes my name, soft and pleading. Her eyes droop as she relaxes into the soft bedding.

"Lara. I'm here." I take her soft hand in my own and give it a gentle squeeze. "I'm not going anywhere."

"Mmhm..." She hums blissfully, watching me through half-lidded eyes. Lara stretches out across the bed like a satisfied feline. Her toes curl and dig into the blankets. I could watch her like this all night, but there's still one thing left to do.

"Lara," I say again, loving the way her name sounds on my tongue. I caress her arms, her face, her neck. She leans into my touch, still floating in the afterglow. My cock aches so badly it hurts, but she's clearly exhausted from her long journey to Aesirheim. They warned us this could be the case, and I -- as usual -- got overzealous.

As I take in the beautiful sight before me, I make my decision. I will not fuck her tonight. Not with my cock, anyway. When I come inside her for the first time, she will be awake and aware of every thrust I give her. But tonight, there's still something I can do...

Reaching down to my trousers, I free my cock and take it in hand while hovering over her. Lara watches me with wide, fucked-out eyes, lips parted in silent awe at my length and girth. Her cute little cunt is so hot, so wet, and so tight. How would it feel gripping me? How would it feel when she comes, clenching and milking my balls dry?

It will be a challenge to fit all of me inside of her, but I'm an Aesir warlord for a reason.

I never back down from a challenge.

I never take my eyes off of her as I start to stroke my cock. The slow, languid pace at first grows into a hotter, more intense passion the more I look at her. The more I take in the sight of her naked body. The shining slick covering her thighs and dampening the bedsheets.

The way her eyes sparkle with a tired bliss I've only ever dreamed of, until now.

She's all mine for the next year. My heart aches when I start to think about what may happen after that, but those thoughts will have to wait. This is a perfect moment, the first night together with my omega, and I will not spoil it for the world.

My hand moves faster and faster, jerking my cock in time with her pants, and already I can see in my mind's eye how she will look full and round with my child. Covered in my seed.

Totally and completely mine.

The thought spurs me over the brink and I yell, clenching the base of my cock as spurt after spurt of hot seed splashes onto her bare belly. I groan, half in pain and half in ecstasy. Never in my life has my release been so mind-blowingly sweet.

Semen drips from my still-leaking cock to her soft skin, and I collapse to the bed beside her. She curls up next to me, as if on instinct, and I wrap one hand possessively around her torso, rubbing my seed into her skin with lazy circles. Lara buries her head in my chest and murmurs something I don't understand, but in this moment, we don't need words. I can understand what she feels well enough.

She will bear my seed and my scent as long as I will have her. And soon, she will bear my child.

Lara snuggles up to me, her small arms light and tender against my own. She lets out a happy sigh and closes her eyes, breaths finally slowing.

I could get used to this. I could really get used to this.

Now that I have her, how will I ever be able to give her up after the year is out?

I don't know, but I'm not going to give her up without a fight. I've known her for less than a day, and already my life feels fuller than it ever has. Could she really be...

My heart-mate?

Lara sleeps so peacefully next to me that I don't want to move a muscle. She must be exhausted -- first from travel, and then from pleasure.

"Sleep, little one," I whisper, brushing a tendril of hair away from her face. I shift ever so slightly in bed so that I can watch over her more carefully, then I lean back and enjoy the calm silence for the first time in what feels like forever. I only have a year.

MORNING AFTER

LARA

I stir awake to brilliant rays of sunlight pouring in from the window. My eyes flit open and I squint against the sudden brightness.

"Janie?" I mutter, rubbing my eyes.

And that's when I remember.

Janie isn't here. Iris neither.

I'm not even on Earth anymore. I'm on an alien planet called Aesirheim, and I just slept with a giant golden alien.

Who, by the way, gave me the best sex of my life. I blush at the memory, my thighs clenching in response. Speaking of...

I roll over in bed and there he is, sitting upright and looking right at me.

"Aah!" I yelp, jumping backward and pulling the blanket around me. "What are you doing?"

Oh, wait, he can't understand me...how am I going to...

"You are very...cute when you sleep. I was simply observing your habits."

Wait a second. I understood that. How did...

His huge golden hand snakes across the covers and cradles my face. With his other hand, he takes my own and lifts it up to cup the left side of my head. I gasp at the small device there, resting over the shell of my ear.

"Your translator," he says. "I fixed it for you while you slept. I hope you do not mind."

My fingers brush over the small device. My stomach lurches for only a moment. I thought it would have to be implanted or something, but it rests over my ear as easily as a pair of glasses.

"Do not worry," Soren continues, as if sensing my concern. "You will not have to wear it forever. It simply interprets the auditory signals and relays them back to the language processing center of your brain. That, and the omega serum you took before embarking here, work in tandem to accelerate language learning. All you have to do is focus..." His face curls up into a knowing grin. "And communicate."

"I..." I stare down at my hands, unsure what to say. Now that I know that he can understand me, I'm second guessing every sentence. What if I say something wrong? What if I offend him -- or worse -- what if he realizes how dull and boring I actually am and decides to call the whole thing off?

"Thank you," I mutter, looking up to give him a soft smile. I grip the covers to pull them aside and get out of bed, but gasp when I realize I'm still naked.

My cheeks flush, the familiar heat building in my groin once more. It's nowhere near the level and intensity of the raging inferno that brought us together last night, but it's a warm, pleasant ache that simmers in the pit of my belly.

"Do not be anxious," Soren says, placing one large hand on my bare shoulder. He gestures at my covered form. "I've already seen everything, remember?" His eyes flash and I swear he throws me a wink, which sends my stomach twisting even further.

"I...uh...I need to go to the bathroom." I gently pull away from his grasp and scoot toward the edge of the bed, covers still wrapped around my body.

"Wait." Soren's voice rumbles through me like thunder, the smallest word burrowing straight to my heart like a shot of liquor.

I look over my shoulder to find he's holding a tablet, not unlike the one I saw Orvox using at orientation.

"I thought you might be hungry after last night, so I took the liberty of researching what foods humans like to eat for breakfast. I wasn't sure what you liked, so I was going to order one of everything, but..."

"What? No!" I snatch the tablet from him.

Soren raises an eyebrow. "What is wrong? Did I do something wrong? I spent all night reading about humans and..."

"No," I assure him. My heart warms at his words. The thought of him staying up, reading how to best take care of me and my needs melts my heart. "This is just...a lot. I'm not used to someone caring about me like this." I trail off, mentally cursing myself. He probably thinks I'm ungrateful, now.

"I am sorry that you feel that way." Soren's voice holds no irritation, only a sad acceptance. "The manner in which you were treated on your home planet is inexcusable. You should not be afraid to ask for what you want and need. You are mine to care for, and I will not let you starve."

My belly gurgles in response, and before I can stop them, tears prick the corners of my eyes. What did I do to deserve this? This was supposed to be a big, scary business transaction. A great sacrifice in order to keep my family safe. But when he acts like that...I might not want to leave.

Swallowing that thought, I distract myself by looking down at the menu on the tablet. My eyes widen. When I see the array of options laid out on the page, my mouth waters even further.

Eggs, bacon, sausage, biscuits, pancakes... the list goes on and on. A spike of homesickness rips through me as I look at the Earth foods. Janie always loved eggs -- over easy, she wouldn't take them any other way -- and Iris loved nibbling on pancakes, the few rare occasions when we had them.

My heart aches. I miss them already, but I know that they'll be well taken care of.

Just like Soren is taking care of me right now.

I pick out a few options then hand the tablet back to Soren with a smile. "I've marked my order on the menu there. That will be enough for now." I stop, chewing my lip before I muster the next words. "Thank you."

Soren gives me a soft, good-natured laugh. "Of course, my dear Lara. It is no concern at all. You are my omega, for the duration of this arrangement. Whatever you desire, it shall be yours." He puts a fist to his chest, bowing his head. "I pledge that to you."

I can only sit there and stare, open mouthed. He's acting like I'm some kind of royalty, but he's the decorated warlord here. Is this...what the entire year will be like?

With a secret smile, I slip out of bed and into the bathroom, feeling the soreness between my thighs.

I wonder what the coming day will bring.

AFTER PANCAKES

SOREN

My Lara is adorable. She lights up with joy at the smallest things, like the plate of Earth pancakes we had delivered. There's one thing I still don't understand about humans, though.

How will she ever have a strong, healthy baby if she eats so little?

Perhaps it is not little for her, I remind myself as we share breakfast together.

I offer her some of my food, but she says she can't handle another bite. I don't want to push her, so I leave it at that, but it looks like I'll need to do some more research.

If she's holding back just because she does not want to offend or inconvenience me, well...that is something I will have to fix. In the meantime, though, I am content to share this meal with her. To finally converse and talk and laugh together.

I have to admit, I was a bit nervous about this whole program. I was unsure if the omega serum would work and I was unsure what Earth girls would even be like. But after last night, I'm a believer.

And what's not to like about the curvy beauty before me? I can hardly tear my eyes away from her. Her hair falls in impossibly soft tresses over her shoulders, still a bit frizzy from sleep. Her dark eyes shine with delight and wonder at my words, at the food, at everything.

If this is luxury to her, it sickens me to know how bad things must have been down on Earth.

I did the right thing. This gorgeous creature deserves nothing less than to be treated like the queen that she is. And what's a small percentage of our wealth and resources to make that a reality?

There are, of course, less noble motivations...

Such as the way she came apart for me last night. The way her face scrunches up in the throes of passion. The delicious nectar between her legs, and the way I get hard just thinking about her. She has no idea what she does to me, and it's a slow, silent torture. I want nothing more than to bend her over the table and fuck her until we're both sweaty and spent.

But I can't. I won't. Not until she's rested and well fed. I owe her that much. Besides, we have the full year left together.

And once she's gotten her strength back, I plan to show her what an Aesir warlord can really do. I will fill her to bursting with my seed. I will mark her and claim her as mine, for the whole planet to see.

Already I know, deep in the pit of my stomach, that one year will not be even close to enough.

After I clean up the dishes from breakfast, I join her in the bedroom. My cock throbs at the mere sight of her by now. It's a painful, but delicious torture I don't think I'll ever get used to. And maybe I don't want to.

Lara lays propped against the pillows, staring at the ceiling with her hands folded. I hate to interrupt her thoughts, but...

"Hello?" I call as I step into the room, tapping gently on the open door.

Lara starts, hands shooting to the covers, then she sees me. A calm, grateful smile breaks through the clouds and lights up the whole room. I thank my lucky stars, once again, for bringing her into my life.

"Hope I wasn't interrupting anything," I say before sitting on the corner of the bed next to her. Is she lying here because she wants me to breed her already? Not that I'm going to say no, but it looks like I still have a lot to learn about human mannerisms.

She shakes her head and scoots up on the bed so that she sits upright. "No, you didn't interrupt anything. I was just thinking." Lara leans forward, taking my hand in both her own. Even with both of her tiny human hands, she's barely able to wrap around my thick palms.

"Oh?" All I know is that I want to keep the conversation going. For her to keep touching me.

"About...everything. About home. About..." She gestures at the cottage. "This."

My stomach drops. She wasn't having second thoughts, was she? They warned us this could happen. Even with the omega serum, sometimes the change was too much for them to handle. We had policies in place in case someone got cold feet, but I didn't expect...

A lump forms in my throat as I let the worries run wild. My Lara. My beautiful Lara. What troubles her so?

The ache in my chest cannot bear to lose her, but if it came down to it...if she truly was unhappy here, and wished to leave...

As much as it would hurt, I would do it.

For her.

Swallowing hard, I shift closer to her. "Is everything all right?" I try to sound as casual as possible. Try not to think about how her answer could change everything.

"Yeah. I'm fine." She wraps her arms around herself, gaze downcast. "I just wanted to say..." Her face flushes the cutest shade of pink I've ever seen. "...thank you. For helping us."

The tension resting on my chest and shoulders takes flight, leaving only a warm relief in its place. I want to tell her that she's more precious than a jewel to me, that any investment seems minuscule next to her presence, but I do my best to keep my voice level. "Of course. It was part of our agreement."

"I don't just mean that." Lara looks up at me, and when she does I see tears flecking the corner of her eyes. "I know you had no way of knowing, but..." She bites her lip. "Things were really bad back on Earth. We barely had enough to eat, and my sister has a two year old, Iris..." She trails off, voice breaking.

I am still learning her language, just as she is with mine, but I don't need to understand every word to feel the emotion. It hits me right in the chest, burning with a pain I didn't know existed. I think back to how she marveled at the food on the breakfast menu. How she lit up at the smallest gesture.

My hands clench into fists and I only barely keep a growl from my throat. The thought of her -- and especially a child -- starving makes me sick to my stomach.

I knew they needed our help, but it didn't sink in just how badly until now. I clasp her hands in return, bowing my head. "You and your loved ones will never go hungry again. Not if I have anything to say about it."

Another, deeper pain twists inside me, but I won't tell her that one. Not yet. The very thought of a small human child fills me with an irrational longing. That is why our people signed the contract with the ISA, after all. Lara may have been starving on her home planet, but we were starving in a very different kind of way.

Starving for new sparks of life.

"If there's ever anything you need, anything at all, I trust that you will tell me. No request is too large." I assure her, brushing stray hairs from her face before leaning down to plant a kiss on her forehead. "I mean it."

Her throat bobs while she works on a response. At last, she gives me a simple, feeble "thank you", but it means more than all the riches in the world coming from her.

Lara sniffs, pulling away before glancing toward the bathroom again.

Do humans make waste that often? I make a mental note to research that, too.

Lucky for me, she has a different idea.

"I was thinking about going to take a shower, so, um..."

I don't let her finish the sentence before she's in my arms, her soft body pressing against mine as I walk her to the bathroom.

SHOWERING

LARA

I don't think I'll ever get used to the feeling of Soren's strong arms around me. Not that I want to. He's so warm and caring and strong...to say nothing of his skills in bed.

I wonder idly if all Aesir are like this. One thing's for certain, though -- I'm pretty sure he's ruined me for human men at this point. How could I go back, knowing what I know now?

Soren, as if sensing my feelings, holds me tighter and presses a gentle kiss to the top of my head. I relax under his touch, my body responding to him in a way that even I don't understand.

First the heat, and now it's like my body is a magnet for his. Like we were made for one another.

How silly that sounds. But what if it's actually the truth? They did say we were matched on a genetic level...

Soren sets me gently on the wide bathroom counter while he steps into the huge shower. I ogled it once earlier, but the longer I look, the more complex and fascinating it is.

Water spouts surround the shower from every imaginable angle, complete with a dizzying set of dials and switches that reminds me more of a pilot's cockpit than a simple shower. Good thing I have Soren here to help me decipher things.

I can't help but chuckle at the thought -- even though the translator's helping me understand his spoken language, the written symbols take a bit longer to digest. If it was just me, I'd probably end up pressing a button for some weird alien slime instead of water and soap.

"Undress." He calls over his shoulder while still working the knobs. Water sprays out from five different spouts, raining down from the ceiling and walls. Steam fills the room shortly, as well as a soft, floral scent that relaxes me all over.

My hands tremble as I slip the robe off of my shoulders and let it fall to the floor. It lands in a puddle of soft cloth at my feet.

"There, everything's adjusted. I'll help you--" Soren straightens and turns to face me, but stops cold when he sees me standing there naked.

His eyes rake a hungry trail from my face down my neck, between my breasts, and down my stomach. I can't help but feel vulnerable under his gaze, but my body sweetens in response, wetness already slicking between my legs.

"Join me," Soren says. He wastes no time pulling off his own clothing, then offering me his hand.

This time I'm the one that's staring. I saw my fill of him last night, of course, but that was in the heat of the moment (literally) and we were so tangled up in bed I didn't get a good look at him. Now, under the bright fluorescent bathroom lights, I can see every inch of his tanned golden skin.

My eyes travel from the wide planes of his shoulders and chest, across his thick arms and small waist, down to the massive cock hanging between his legs.

Massive. That's the only word for it. My mouth waters as I take it in. My core clenches in response, the all-too-familiar heat rising once more. It's as thick as my forearm and impossibly long. I suck in breath and jerk my gaze back upward to his face.

How on Earth is that thing going to fit inside of me?

It twitches, almost in response. My hands itch to fondle and caress it. My mouth waters, my stomach tenses. Not to mention the crease between my legs pulsing and quivering in time with every frantic beat of my heart.

"See something you like?" He muses, his smirk sending another rush of shame and pleasure racing through my veins.

I lick my lips, step forward, and take his hand. He helps me into the shower, then joins me and closes the door behind us.

If the shower looked luxurious from the outside, it's nothing compared to what it feels like to be under the steaming streams. The water pressure pounds into my sore muscles, working away the knots and washing away the grime of my journey.

The scent of lavender and soap fills the enclosed space, but there's something else there, too. The smell of *him*. Soren stands tall and impossibly broad before me, blocking the spray when he moves to press a button for soap. He lathers it in both his hands before turning to me. "Come. Let me wash you."

I pull my hair away from the back of my neck, and he begins.

The soap-slicked palms of his hands glide across my shoulders and up my neck. He washes my arms, then my neck and cleavage before sliding his hands lower to cup my breasts.

Soren's touch is gentle, but firm. My nipples harden immediately, pressing against his palms. I gasp, my breath hitching. I can't help it, even though I know he's barely begun.

He moves his hands more firmly across my breasts, squeezing and rubbing the soft skin. I moan, arching my back and pressing them even more firmly against his hands. Soren chuckles, but he doesn't stop the delicious torment.

"I know it feels good," He whispers, "but I'm only just starting. Let me wash you all over."

I nod, shivering. His hands continue down my body, caressing me all over, paying special attention to every sweet spot. No one's ever washed me before. Especially not like this.

I sigh and lean into him while he works his magic. The soaps and lotions glide over my skin and Soren's hands are everywhere, my skin hot and tight in his wake. The heat from the shower and the heat from my body combine to create a heady, hazy state of arousal that feels like a dream.

Soren works his way down my body, paying attention to every curve and crevice. He slicks down my legs and then back up, painfully slow, until he cups the curve of my ass. I suck in a breath and cling to his broad, wet chest, unable to control the sensations any longer.

His strong, wide hands massage the globes of my ass, inching closer and closer to my slit with each pass. I bite my lip, trying to hide a moan, but he chuckles against me.

"What's the matter? I'm simply trying to make sure you are clean." He rinses his hands of soap and presses further, fingers brushing against my entrance. I bury my head in his chest, letting out a shameful whimper.

"You are so wet for me," he murmurs, breath hot and tingly against my ear.

"Y-yes," I gasp. He pushes his hand between my legs and parts them further, holding my upper body steady. Soren's deft fingers slide across my slick folds before circling the nub of pleasure at my apex. I let out another whimper and my knees tremble.

"Your fingers," I whisper between shaky breaths, "so big..."

"Is that so?" He murmurs against the spray. "You're going to be taking a lot more than just my fingers, love."

This time I can't hold back a moan. I melt into his touch, letting his fingers work their way deeper. Soren's thumb comes to rest on my clit, flicking tight circles as his fingers curl inside me. I thrash and cling to him for dear life, unsure if the blistering heat is from the shower or the slick friction of our bodies.

"Lara," he pants, using his other hand to take my chin and tilt it up toward his own. "Kiss me."

There's no mistaking the pure, primal lust written all over his face. If I wasn't hopelessly turned on already, that did me in. I revel in the thought that I, a simple human girl, has such an effect on a huge alien warlord. It's a heady, intoxicating sort of power, and I can't get enough.

I want to be the cause of his delighted sighs. The reason he thrusts and trembles beneath me. I want to give him everything just as he's given me.

But surely, that must be the omega serum talking. I barely know the guy, and yet...

"Kiss me," Soren rumbles again, and those skeptical thoughts wash away with the spray. I run my hand through his hair on the back of his neck and pull him down to me, claiming his lips with my own.

My body tightens and I moan into his mouth at the contact, but I'm not the only one. He returns my moan with one of his own, sucking on my lower lip while he pounds his fingers into me with more and more urgency. His cock twitches against my stomach and for a second I think he's about to take me right there in the shower.

He takes my hand and guides it to his cock, letting me feel the slick hardness of his shaft. I gasp and run my hands up and down the shaft. It's much like a human's, except for the raised ridges on the underside. I shudder to think how they will feel, grinding against my most sensitive areas. Will he even fit? Will he split me in half? Will I cry, and will it be from pleasure or pain?

Part of me is still nervous and confused about all these changes and feelings I'm going through. But another part of me -- a bigger part -- wants to see just how much more he has to offer.

Soren's fingers quicken even as I grind against him. The world is a swirl of steam, heat, and pleasure. It shrinks and shrinks until it's just us, just him, and the sparks that connect us with every touch, every kiss, every grunt and moan and cry...

And then he rips away to press a bruising kiss to the side of my neck and I come, screaming out his name as I spasm around him. Waves of pleasure ripple through me, soothing some of the burn but leaving even more in its place. It's not enough. It will never be enough when I'm with him.

Luckily he senses the same thing because he pulls away, licking his lips as he turns off the shower.

"So sweet," he rasps, "So delicious. You taste better than the finest Aesir wine."

I have no idea how to respond to that, but I don't have to. My body does the talking.

"Come, Lara," Soren motions for me to take his hand. He guides us out of the shower and grabs a fluffy bath towel that's larger than I am, wrapping it around my shoulders.

I dry off as quickly as I can while Soren does the same. From the urgency of both our movements, I know we're not even close to done. Because one thing, one word still lingers in the back of my mind, echoing every second that we're together. Reminding me why I'm here in the first place.

Breed.

"Come, Lara." He says again, and this time his words hold all the weight in the world. "It is time."

MATING

SOREN

I promised myself when I signed the contract that I would do this right. That I would give this woman -- this omega -- the attention and passion she deserved. Only then would I lay with her. Only then would I fuck her to bursting with my seed.

I did my part. I waited as long as I could, and I'm proud of myself for that. Though my hormones shout at me to ravish her like a wild animal, I've been soft and gentle up until now. My precious Lara has eaten, rested, and bathed.

Now it's time for the main event.

I carry her still-damp body to the bed, throwing off the blankets and extra pillows. This time, there will be nothing to get in our way.

She mewls so softly, so sweetly as I lay her down on the mattress. Her freshly showered hair spreads out around her head like a halo and damn near takes my breath away. Her dark lips part in wonder and she looks up at me, eyes brimming with barely controlled lust.

That makes two of us.

I crawl to her on hands and knees, admiring each line and curve of her naked body. I kiss my way up her supple thighs. Her round hips. Her soft, sensitive breasts. But this time, I don't have to stop there.

This time, she will fully know what it is to make love the Aesir way.

Taking soft handfuls of her shapely thighs, I part them to make room for me. The smell of her arousal hits me stronger than ever, sending my already frantic heart rate into overdrive.

I can't wait any longer. I have to have her.

Now.

"Lara, look at me. I'm going to be as gentle as I can, but -- ahh -- you have to let me know if I'm hurting you. All right?"

She nods silently, chest rising and falling with her shuddering breaths.

"I need to hear you say it." My voice teeters on the brink of control. I know she signed the contract. We both did. But here, in the moment of truth, what she says next means everything. As much as I crave her, I cannot bear to cause her any pain. I need to know that she needs this just as badly as I do.

Lara shivers beneath my touch, her eyes glassy and unfocused. She weaves a hand around my waist and another to the side of my face. "Yes, Soren..." It's barely more than a whisper, but that's all I need. "Breed me." She shudders again, heat and scent pouring off of her in drowning waves. "A-alpha. Breed me. Please."

With that, the last vestige of control shatters. She's mine.

I lift up her legs and rest them on my shoulders, leaning forward to line up my cock with her entrance. She's wet -- seeping, dripping wet, so much that she's already staining the bed sheets -- but that's the least of my concerns. I don't take my eyes off of her face as I press the head of my cock past her folds.

Her eyes open wide in shock and probably pain. I stop moving, waiting for her pinched face to go away. For her muscles to soften around me.

"Relax," I soothe her, leaning forward to caress her cheek as she gets used to me. "You can take it. Your body was made for this. For me."

The words seem to have an instantaneous effect on her. She lets out a soft moan and melts into the bed. Her pussy lips suck my cock in deeper, already so hot and tight. Fuck, she feels incredible and we've barely even started. My balls tighten against my body, readying the torrent of seed that will soon grow new life.

But not yet. Not yet. I have a woman to please first.

"Are you all right?" I whisper.

She nods, eyes clouded with lust and want. Her hips twitch upward in response, forcing my cock deeper into her pussy. Guess that answers my question.

"I need...more. Please."

"And who am I to deny my omega?" I growl, giving her hips a squeeze. "You can have everything, Lara. Everything."

Running my hands down her thighs, I lean back slightly for a better angle and press upward. Her walls contract around me and she wails.

"Ah...Soren!"

And what music my name on her lips is. The sweetest symphony I've ever heard. I thrust a little deeper, watching her expression, relishing her cries.

I had no idea humans were so...expressive. And I know, now that I have her, that I'll never get enough.

We build up a gentle rhythm, slow at first as she takes my huge cock inch by inch. I soothe and praise and caress her through it all, and before either of us know it, my hips are up against hers.

"Lara," I breathe before leaning down for a kiss. "My girl, my good, good girl...you've taken me whole. I told you you could do it."

"Ah..." she mumbles, words slurred by lust and eyes half-lidded. "Yes, don't stop...Soren. Don't stop, please..." Her walls clench around me, hanging on so tightly like they're afraid to let go. Like they know I belong here, deep in her pussy. I run my thumb over her clit, flicking it in soft, staggered strokes that leave her writhing. Each thrust I press down on her nub a bit more. Every time our bodies meet, I grunt and groan and let my instincts take over.

Mine. Mine mine mine. She's going to take my cock. My seed. And then, after she swells huge and heavy, she will bear my child.

I lean down to suckle her dark nipples and she wraps her small arms around my shoulders and neck, nails digging into my flesh as she trembles and cries out. The sounds morph together into a constant litany of pleasure and I focus on one nipple, then the other, while driving deeper with every thrust and grinding against her needy, swollen clit.

"Yes...oh god, yes! Soren, Soren, don't stop...please don't stop! I'm gonna --"

As I suck her left breast into my mouth and dig in with my teeth, she comes undone, crying out my name as her walls spasm around me. Fuck, if I thought she was tight before!

She clamps down around me, milking my cock like a vise, and it's all I can do to keep from following her over that precipice. I don't want to come yet. Not when she's still so beautiful, so soft and sweet and pliant in my arms. I want to hear her cries for the rest of the night. Want to bathe her in my scent and mark her with my cum.

"Fuck!" I yell, pulling out and gripping her hips, flipping her over so her round ass faces me. Her eyes widen with surprise, but she doesn't hesitate to spread her shaking legs and lift her hips for me.

"Good girl," I growl, thrusting back into her beautiful wetness once more.

The sound she makes -- somewhere between a yelp and a moan -- tells me everything I need to know. She might be from another planet, but she was *made* for me. I feel it in my heart and I feel it in my soul, deeper down than I've ever felt anything. This is it. This is her. The one I've been waiting for.

My heart-mate.

Mine.

I grab on to her round, baby-making hips and pull her to me, again and again as I thrust deeper and deeper. Lara buries her face, panting and moaning while her hands fist the sheets.

My alpha instinct roars to the surface in full force and I can't hold back any longer. The sounds of our shouts and our slick bodies fill the room as I pound into her, hitting every sensitive spot she has. I rain spank after spank on her perfect ass, one to match each delicious moan I wrench out of her.

And she loves it, too, her voice growing higher, her pussy clenching in time with my thrusts and my spanks. I can't help but grin to myself. What did I do to get so lucky?

When I find out how much she likes being spanked, I start to experiment. A smack here, a spank there, interspersing them with quick, violent thrusts that shake the bed and leave her gasping for breath. She's getting close again, I can tell, but --

"Not yet." I pull out again and lay her down on her back, gazing into her beautiful eyes. "I'm going to fuck my way deep inside you now, Lara. I'm going to come inside you, and I want to see your face as I fill you up."

She rests her hands on either side of my face, her expression only one of blissed out reverence. "Yes..." she whimpers, barely audible. "I need it, please...your cum..."

"With pleasure, my omega. I'm going to pump so much cum into you that you won't be able to hold it all. You'll be leaking cum for days after this, and you won't be able to take a single step without thinking of me. I'm going to put a baby inside you, Lara. I'm going to make you the mother of my child."

All my walls and inhibitions fall away as I give myself over to the pleasure. I pump into her, deeper and harder and faster than before. Gone are my worries about hurting her -- to my surprise she meets me thrust for thrust, her eyes never leaving mine. And when I finally reach that sacred crescendo, I hold her closer than I've ever held anything in my life and force out a ragged whisper.

"Come for me, Lara. Together!"

"Soren!" Her whole body shudders as she loses herself one more time. Wave after wave of hot, sticky cum floods her fertile womb, oozing out around her lips and pooling onto the bed. I collapse on top of her, our bodies still connected and smeared with sweat and cum, and we lie there together, trying to catch our breaths.

For a single, blessed moment there's only the sounds of our breathing, rising and falling as we bask in the afterglow. I prop myself up on one elbow and take in the sight of her.

She's sweaty and spent, but I can tell by the blissful look in her eyes that she is oh so satisfied. The yearning in my chest grows the longer I stay here next to her. I knew that the changes in our bodies drove us to mate, but we had done so. This was something different.

No longer the desperate inferno of lust that threatened to consume me. This was a softer, gentler warmth that started in my heart and spread outward. It felt...safe, somehow?

Like I was finally somewhere I belonged. Like all those long years of war and fighting and losing men I called brothers were worth it.

I closed my eyes against the thought and shook it from my mind. There would be time for questions later. We had plenty of time to explore one another. For now, I would be content simply holding her close to me. Lara's breaths even out as she drifts asleep and relaxes against me. My fingers draw lazy patterns over her bare skin. I smear the remaining cum that dribbles out across her breasts, her neck, her womb.

When she wakes up, she will be marked with my scent. I'd like to see any other male try to take her now. The whole planet will know -- and

Lara will know, too -- that she is completely and irrevocably mine.

Just as much as I am hers.

My cock throbs as I drift my fingers over her stomach. Thoughts of a healthy, happy baby fill my brain and warm my heart. Another primal urge washes over me and I grip my cock, wanting to take her again. When she turns her head in her sleep and I see her soft, peaceful face, I relax.

For now, I will let her rest.

But let's just say I know the perfect way to wake her later.

CRAVING THE OUTDOORS

LARA

TWO WEEKS LATER

Who knew an alien could be such a great lover?

I sit up in bed, propped up against countless fluffy pillows, while I play with the settings on the video wall. Next to me sits a half-eaten box of chocolates. Outside the windows a scene right out of a postcard takes place.

Well, if that postcard were from space.

The sky flames with purples and reds and even some greens, so much more vibrant than the colors on Earth. It feels closer, somehow. Fuller. Their moon hangs just above the horizon, a thin halo only barely visible. Towering cliffs and lush forests surround us with so much natural beauty I don't know where to look first. Already I can hear the ekkori, as Soren calls them, come out of the ground and light up the night with their luminescent bodies.

Alien fireflies -- who knew?

I turn off the video wall and draw my legs to my chest. Even though it has been only a short time, I feel like I'm starting to get used to life here on Aesir.

My body has adjusted to the omega serum; my weekly checkups are looking good. They only take a minute or two to scan my vitals, but you should see Soren's face. He glowers and looms over them until the tech leaves, snarling in their wake.

He's got a possessive streak a mile wide, but if I'm being honest? I don't mind it so much. In fact, I kind of love it.

Back on Earth, I had so many responsibilities I never had much time to date. And even when I did, no one had ever put me first the way Soren did.

I pop another chocolate into my mouth and lay back on the pillows, staring up at the ceiling. There's a lofted skylight so we can view the stars, and already they're starting to shine through in little diamonds of light. I always loved stargazing as a child. I'd look up there and beg my mom to tell me the name of every constellation and every star. She didn't know most of them, so we started making up our own. It was a game we used to play, up until she passed away. My heart aches at the thought. I wonder what she would think if she knew I was on another planet, contracted to have a baby with an alien warlord? What would she think of Soren?

My thoughts drift and I wonder idly how the other women from the program are doing. Are their mates just as attentive and caring as Soren? Are they being taken care of?

My core clenches at the thought. 'Taken care of' is one way to describe how Soren's treated me, but it's not nearly enough. He goes above and beyond in every way to ensure that I'm happy, well-rested, well-fed, and most of all -- well-fucked.

I let out a soft moan at the thought, my hand drifting lower. I knew that coming here to be a surrogate meant I'd have to have sex, but I guess I didn't realize just how much of it I'd be having.

Not that I'm complaining -- Soren's the best lover a girl could ask for. He brings me to the brink again and again until I'm brainless and blissed out beneath him. Only then does he take his pleasure, pumping me full of cum until I can't hold any more.

The mere sight of him, the mere scent, is enough to get me going these days. I've never been so sensitive in my life. While it's nothing like the all-consuming heat that took me when I arrived, it's always there.

Waiting for his touch. His kiss. His cock.

Thankfully, I never have to wait long.

We started to mix it up after the first week. Sometimes he finishes inside me. Sometimes he will finish on my chest or in my mouth. That last one is secretly my favorite. Who knew alien cum tasted so good?

I love the way his pupils blow wide when I finger myself with his cum, pushing it deeper and deeper into my pussy. When I'm through, I'll lick each finger clean, and I swear the look on his face starts the cycle of lust all over again.

But as great as sex with Soren is, I'm starting to get a bit bored in the cottage all day. Soren wanted me to stay here for the first two weeks so we could get acclimated, but it's been more than enough time. My legs itch to get out and explore. There's a whole alien world just outside that door, and I intend to learn as much about it as I can.

Soren appears in the doorway and startles me from my thoughts. I shove the chocolate box behind my back and give him a smile.

"Hey," he says, leaning against the doorframe. I don't think I'll ever get used to the size difference between us. He positively looms in the doorway, head reaching all the way to the top, while I feel like I'm in a cottage made for giants. "How's my beautiful omega doing?"

A blush rises to my cheeks at his words. At first, I didn't like being called that. I worried that it reduced me to no more than my hormones or my physical reactions. But as time went on, I realized that he didn't mean it in a disparaging way. It was his method of showing just how important I was to him.

"I'm fine," I say, stretching and slipping out of bed. I walk over and wrap my arms around him. His body heat both excites and calms me in the most paradoxical way, but when he smells this good...

I nuzzle into his chest and then look up at him. He leans down to kiss me, his lips hot and possessive against mine. I feel him swell against me, but as nice as that sounds...

"I want to go out today." I spit the words a bit too fast, worried that I'll have second thoughts if I wait too long. His eyes widen for a fraction of a second.

"Out?" He raises an eyebrow. "But you have everything you could ever want here." Soren pauses. "Unless there's something I'm missing? Whatever it is, say the word and I'll get it for you."

I press my hands against his chest and push away. His insistence on spoiling me is so charming, but that's not what I need right now. "I've been in this cottage ever since you came to get me. I want to know what it's like out there." I step toward the huge windows and peer out, palms flat against the glass. "I came all the way from Earth, Soren. You don't understand -- we don't have anything like this. Not even close."

Soren snorts. "Sounds boring."

"It's beautiful in its own way." My heart swells with homesickness once again. I think of Janie and Iris down on Earth, and send out a silent prayer for their health. I know they are doing better now with the stipend from the ISA, but I can't help but worry. They're my family, after all.

A flutter of movement catches my eye as I look out upon the small valley. My alien mate comes up behind me and wraps his hands around my waist. His bulk against mine feels right. Feels safe. But he's not going to change the subject that easily.

"What's that?" I ask, pointing to a small creature scampering out of the trees into the grassy area. A long white streak runs down its otherwise dark colored back. It trots along on four legs, making its way to a small stream.

"That's a masaka. Cute little devils, but they don't much care for people. They're nocturnal. It's rare to see one out and about like this. They prefer to live underground."

"Wow." My mind spins with the new information. "And what's that? Is that a giant mushroom?" Down near the stream a huge, round-topped fungus blocks out the moonlight.

"Mushroom." He mulls over the word for a moment. "Yes, I believe that is what your people would call them. To us they are known as fintus."

"So cool..." I turn away from the window to give him my best cute puppy-dog face. "Can we go out and explore? I want you to show me around. Can we do that?"

Soren opens his mouth as if to protest, but thinks better of it. He cups my cheek with his large golden hand and smiles. "Yes. But not tonight."

"Tomorrow?"

"Not tomorrow."

"Ugh!" I groan. "Why are you keeping me here like this? I thought I could have whatever I wanted. And what I want is to go outside."

Soren holds up his hands and takes a step backward. Is the fearsome alien warlord actually...backpedaling? "It's not that I don't want to! It's just..." He rubs the back of his neck.

"The first two weeks are critical for your body to acclimate to the new environment. And after the omega serum made you go into heat, I kept you here to keep you safe. According to my research, the hormone levels should fluctuate back toward normal levels in the next few days. And then, I promise, I will show you all the sights and sounds of Aesir." His lips form a thin smile, but it doesn't reach his eyes.

"There's something else." I cross my arms. "What's on your mind?"

Soren lets out a breath. "Soon we'll know if all that baby-making worked or not."

I flush at his words. My clit twitches up against my body and my walls contract. Oh, I remember the baby-making, all right. I'll remember those days and nights of pleasure until the day I die.

Of course, it wasn't just for pleasure. A mental image of Soren carrying a swaddled baby bundle jumps into my mind. Of Soren feeding the little one. Of tiny fingers and tiny toes reaching out for him. He's so kind and gentle despite his size and power. He would be a great father. I just know it.

So why does my heart already ache at the thought of leaving him and our child?

"What if it doesn't...take? We can try again, right? We have the whole year."

The more I think about it, the more I realize how anxious I am. I came here on contract to have a baby for this alien warlord. And if I can't do that...do I forfeit the contract? Will they send me back home? Cut off our funding? My stomach twists into a knot.

No. I can't let that happen.

We had sex on practically every surface, in practically every position, multiple times a day for the last two weeks. Surely one of those times he knocked me up.

Right?

Soren steps toward me again, placing a hand on my still-flat stomach. "We have the year, yes, but we have to allow time for gestation." He makes a sound deep in his chest, almost like a muted growl. "The window is...very small."

"It'll happen," I promise him with a conviction I don't feel. I slip my hands over his and give them a squeeze.

"I hope so."

And as I stare out across the moon-light plains of an alien landscape, I hope so too.

SPANKING IN THE STABLE

LARA

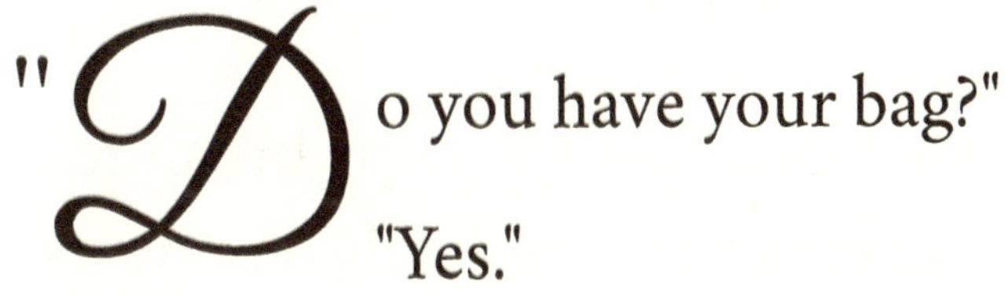

"Do you have your bag?"

"Yes."

"Your sunscreen?"

"Yes, now can we --"

"Your communicator in case we get separated?"

"Soren!"

After what feels like forever, I'm getting ready to leave the cottage for the first time and explore Aesir. The only problem is, Mr. Worrywart Alpha is fussing over every little thing.

"All right, all right. Fine." He holds his hands up. "I surrender."

That makes me snort. "You, the fabled warlord? Surrendering so easily?"

He leans closer until his lips brush my ear. "If I remember correctly, you were the one surrendering last night." I gasp at his brash words. I should be used to them by now, but they catch me off guard every time.

"Shut up." I smile and give him a playful nudge. "Now come on. Let's go."

"After you." He taps in a code on the keypad and at long last, the door swishes open.

A rush of fresh air greets me like the sweetest summer wind. It blows my gauzy white dress behind me, clinging to my breasts and hips. A long slit up each side provides for easy movement, but it almost reveals a startling amount of skin if not for the comfortable pants that I'm wearing underneath the dress. Still, Soren tells me this is how they dress here.

When on Aesir, do as the Aesir do.

He locks the door and joins me in the garden. He cuts quite the dapper figure himself -- tight black pants tucked into sturdy boots. A fitted sleeveless shirt shows off his impressive muscles. When he walks past me and motions for me to follow, my mouth practically waters at the sight of his fine ass.

But there will be plenty of time for that later. I wanted to go on a tour today, and I'm not going to let anything get in the way of that.

When we reach the gate, I link my fingers with his and look out at the trails leading away from the cottages and back the way we came. "Are we going back to the center?" I ask as we walk.

"No," he says. "Not at first, anyway. There's something I want to show you."

"What is it?" I have to crane my neck to make eye contact, so I shield my eyes from the glaring sun with my free hand.

Soren's golden face twitches upward into a grin. "A surprise."

I huff in amusement. "Fine. Keep your secrets. But it's not far, right?"

"Not far."

We walk for a few more minutes in comfortable silence. I point out strange and wonderful new plants and formations, and Soren tells me all about them with pride. He looks so in his element like this. So proud of his homeland.

I can understand why they fought so hard to protect it, now.

And why I'm fighting so hard for my family.

Time flies when I'm with him. We walk and talk and laugh as the trail leads on and on. The wide world of Aesir spreads out around us, and each new sight fills me with awe all over again. This place really is beautiful.

I look up at Soren and catch him looking at me. He smiles and squeezes my hand, and I realize...I'm happy here.

"We're almost there," he says. "Shall we?"

"Lead on."

So hand-in-hand, we continue down the trail together.

A large wooden building comes into view. For once, something familiar. I'd know that shape anywhere.

A stable. We duck into the cavernous space -- well, Soren ducks because he's so tall. Light filters in from evenly placed slats in the ceiling. I think to myself as we walk among the stalls, at least this is one thing that hasn't changed.

They're largely unoccupied and I'm starting to think the stable's abandoned when we come to the end of the walkway. There, head bowed and chewing on a mouthful of hay, is one of those deer-horse creatures again.

An aki, he called them?

But when it raises its proud head and looks right at us, even I can recognize the intensity of the gaze. That's the same animal that carried us to the cottage to begin with.

"After you pointed out practically every living thing on Aesir, I thought you might want to meet Caltryx." Soren reaches his hand over the gate and Caltryx walks up to meet him. I expected some sort of nuzzling action, but what happens is more akin to a head butt. I gasp and stumble backward, but Soren simply laughs.

Was that what was supposed to happen?

"Oh, don't worry about her," Soren says, patting her neck now. "It's a game we like to play with one another."

"You guys...know each other?" It sounds idiotic as soon as it comes out of my mouth, but I don't know how else to ask it.

He chuckles in response. "You could say that. She and I share a very special bond. It goes beyond just mount and rider. We...share everything."

I furrow my brow. "Everything? Like, you can read minds and stuff?"

Soren shakes his head. "No. Not like that. But we have been together for so long, our souls resonate with one another. I can tell how she's feeling, even if we're apart. As she can with me."

I don't miss the prideful gleam in his eye. He looks upon his mount the way a father may look upon his child. My hand shoots to my stomach at the thought. If he looked even half as enamored with *our* child...

He was going to make an excellent father.

"I've raised her since she was a week old, you know. We've seen a lot together. If it weren't for Cali here, I'd have been dead in battle ages ago." Soren lovingly pets her fur, then gestures to me. "Come on, don't be shy."

I hesitate. "She's not going to, um...do that head butt thing with me, right? That's fine for you, but I'd rather not be launched across the stable."

"She knows you are special to me." That's his only answer, but it's enough. The warm feeling of hope and happiness spreads through my heart and chest before moving down to my belly.

He would never hurt me. And neither would Cali.

So I take a deep breath, raise my hand, and step toward the creature with wide eyes. Cali makes a low snorting sound, then nudges her snout against my hand. A long, pink tongue shoots out and leaves my wrist covered in saliva. I pull back, laughing.

"That tickles!"

"That means she likes you," Soren says proudly. "Believe it or not, she's not this friendly with everyone. She won't go near my comrades."

Something about that sends a surge of pride through myself as well. I remember back when I first got here, when Soren threw me on Cali's back before I could even talk to him. I remember how smooth the ride was, and how warm Soren was at my back.

"What an incredible creature," I say, awestruck.

"I like to think so."

I look up when I hear voices outside the door. They're the first other people I've seen in weeks! Another huge, looming golden alien stalks through the stable without so much as a glance at us, but that's not what I'm interested in. One of the other women from Earth is with him!

In my excitement, I call out and wave to her, rushing forward to say hi. As amazing as this alien planet is, it's such a relief to see another human!

I don't make it very far, however, before a strong arm wraps around my middle and yanks me back toward the stall. "Hey!" I cry out, looking up at him to demand an answer. "What was that about?"

Soren's hard gaze follows the other man. His grip tightens. I slap his hand on my stomach. "This is silly. I just want to say hello. Let me go!"

Apparently that's the wrong answer. He whirls me around to face him, a menacing growl rumbling up from his chest. I see for the first time what looks like displeasure in his eyes. What did I do?

"Hey!" I yell again, but he wraps his free hand around my mouth, too. What the hell?!

I hear voices behind me, but they fade away with the long, lumbering foot-steps of another mount. When the door creaks open and they are out of earshot, Soren releases me.

My hands drop to my sides and clench into fists. Heat burns my cheeks, and not the good kind. "What was --"

I don't get a chance to finish my sentence. He hauls me into the stall and closes the door behind us.

Cali stands beside us, a silent witness to the fiasco unfolding before me. There's no one to call for help. No one close enough to hear.

"Put your hands on the gate." Soren's voice is deeper and scarier than I've ever heard it.

"What? I'm not going to --"

One hand lands on the middle of my back. The other around my waist. He pushes me down roughly until my hands brace against the wooden gate. My heart stutters in my chest, but it's not entirely from fear. There's something about the way he manhandles me, the commanding tone in his voice, that speaks to the primal urges deep inside.

I'm not actually getting turned on by this, am I?

"We can do this the easy way," his hand runs down the small of my back until it rests across my ass. "Or the hard way." At his words, his other hand wraps around to gently rest around my throat.

"Spread your legs."

I suck in a breath.

"Now." His boot knocks against my left ankle and I bow even further, bent double against the stable door while he has a full view of my behind. My dress and pants still cover my butt, but knowing him, not for long...

"Do you know why I'm doing this, Lara?" Soren's voice loses some of its edge, but there's still more than enough to make my core twitch in anticipation.

I shiver. I try to fight it, but I can't. No more than I can fight Soren's all-consuming presence. Already I can feel how wet I am down there, and it's only getting worse the more he touches me.

Damn him.

"I asked you a question," he says, the hand on my throat tightening ever so slightly.

"N-no," I manage to sputter out. And it's the truth. I really don't know. One moment we were bonding with Cali, and then the others came in and suddenly...

This.

"I don't know how you do things on your planet, but while you're here, you play by our rules. I'm sure you're aware of my position as warlord. And because of that, I have a certain reputation to upkeep among my men. Do you understand?"

I furrow my brow and try to piece together the answers amidst the haze of lust and humiliation. Is he ashamed to be seen with me? Is that it?

Soren's hand brushes across my ass and down my legs until he reaches the hem of my dress. He hikes it up in a single fluid motion, and all I can do is lean against the gate and wait for what happens next. He rips my pants off of me.

The hand on my throat moves down to my chest and grabs at my breast, pinching the nipple. I cry out and while I'm still processing the sudden movement, a loud smack rains down on my ass.

The combination of pleasure and pain catches me off guard and I let out a shuddering moan.

"You are being punished for questioning me in front of one of my men. Understand that what we do in our private quarters is different from the manner I must display myself in public."

My eyes widen as his fingers slip into my panties and slip them down over my legs. He stops at the knees, the sodden panties practically binding my legs.

"Fuck, you're so wet down here." He swipes a finger across my folds as I hiss in a breath. "Don't tell me that you've been this desperate for me all morning." His low, rumbling laugh turns my knees to jelly.

"You wish," I whisper. I try to remember to breathe. In through my nose, out through my mouth. In, out.

And then he spanks me again. The fresh sting races across my skin and another shameful rush of arousal gathers between my thighs. Hot, slick liquid coats his fingers and he brings them up to his face, sniffing and then licking them.

"I do wish," he says.

I try and look at him over my shoulder, but he forces my head back down. I mumble a protest but my panties are still around my knees. I can't very well hobble off like this.

"But right now, what I wish is for you to learn your place." Soren caresses the tender, still stinging skin before smacking it again. Once, twice, three times. I bite my lip and try not to flinch or cry out, but each strike sends me higher and higher.

It's not long before any thought of defiance or brattiness vanishes from my mind. I'm so in tune with my body and the sensations Soren gives me that there's no room for anything else. I slump against the stable door, moaning with wild abandon as he spanks my ass again and again. Heat floods off the reddened, tired skin, but he doesn't stop.

Tears prick to my eyes and everything mutes together into a hazy blur. Endorphins flood my system and a chill races from head to toe. Every cell on my body is alive and tingling.

"You like this, don't you?" Soren leans forward to whisper in my ear. "Which part of it turns you on the most -- the humiliation or the pain?" Another spank. "Or perhaps its the rough treatment that gets you off. Is that it?" Spank. "Fuck, I wonder if you could come from this."

"Mmm." I can't manage much but pants and moans at this point. My whole body is on fire with both pain and pleasure. I'm so close, so deliriously close to release. And he must know it, too.

The spanking wasn't the real punishment.

The edging is.

Every blow makes my pussy clench tighter. My climax rears its head, ready to drag me under, but it's just there, almost, almost...

I push into him. My back arches lewdly as I'm bent double in the stable, being disciplined like a naughty child, and yet it's still not enough.

Soren picks up on my quickening breath and slows his strokes, chuckling to himself. I hiss and slump bonelessly against him and the stable, but my climax evades me once more.

"Soren!" I cry out. I'm not above begging at this point. "I'm sorry, just...fuck!" My hips thrust backward into empty air and I'm clawing at the wood, chasing something I can't reach alone.

"Let me come," I pant like a prayer. "Oh, Soren, let me come please."

He rubs his wide hands over my bottom, the skin still burning and red. It will be for some time, and I'll definitely notice the next time I try to sit down. Was that what he intended?

"What have we learned?" Soren asks. He brushes the fallen strands of hair away from my sweaty face. Caresses my cheeks. It's soft and fulfilling and wholesome, but it's not what I crave, and he knows it.

"I...mm..." The world spins while my brain tries to form words. "That you're the alpha. That you...have to be in command. That I...embarrassed you."

Soren hums in approval, one hand stroking my back possessively while the other cups the burning globes of my ass. "See, was that so hard?"

I huff out a breath and stay silent. He's messing with my head again, but damn if it doesn't send my instincts into overdrive.

"And it looks like," Soren muses, hands gently ghosting over my sore behind, "you've uncovered something new about yourself, haven't you, Lara?"

I close my eyes. I know my face -- no, my whole body -- flushes with shame and arousal, but I can't help it. The truth of my desire is written on my body, plain for the world to see.

"Shall we do that again, sometime?" He ponders. Just the thought of it makes me twitch in anticipation. I don't want to say anything, but if I don't...

"Or perhaps you don't like it, after all. Perhaps you wish I'd never redden your naughty bottom ever again, until you're breathless and begging for my cock..."

"No," I rasp out. "Don't."

"Oh?" He slips a finger between my cheeks and down to my slit. I know what he'll find there, but that doesn't make it any less humiliating. I welcome the intrusion of his thick, calloused finger like an old friend. He covers his finger in my juices and draws away, looking at it for a moment. "Do my eyes deceive me, then? Or were you not dripping all over yourself just from me spanking you?"

I bite my lip and look away. So much for getting out of this with my dignity intact. "I meant..."

He maneuvers around to hover his thumb over my throbbing clit. "Use your words, darling, or you're going to be stuck like this for a very long time."

"I meant..." I hang my head. "Don't stop...doing it. Please. I don't care. Just...keep touching me. Please. I need it. Soren." I glance at him over my shoulder, eyes shining with lust and unshed tears.

Something changes in his expression just then, clicking into place like a key in a lock. "There we go," he coos, pressing down on my engorged clit and leaning forward. His hot, muscular torso presses against my back. Soren's cock stands at full mast, already bobbing against my wetness. "See what happens when you're a good girl for me?"

He wraps one hand around my hair and pulls gently so that my head tilts back. "Now this good girl's gonna get her reward."

And with one hand clenching my hips and the other bowing my back upward toward him, he slams himself inside me.

My whole body jerks forward and I almost lose my balance, if not for Soren's strong grip holding me in place.

"If you behave, I'll make sure to fuck you like this every day." Soren kisses the back of my neck and then bites down, hard enough to leave a mark. "Wouldn't that be nice?" He murmurs between kisses and licks of my fevered skin. "I can make you feel so good. Mix the pleasure and pain until you cannot discern where one ends and the other begins."

And right now, in the moment?

There's nothing I'd like more.

He pulls back and then rams into me again. Again. Again. There's a rhythm to the way his hips slap against my sore bottom, and I can feel every inch and ridge of his cock stretching my most sensitive places. It doesn't take long for that fire to return, smoldering with a vengeance and reaching higher and higher still...

"Ah...fuck, Soren, I'm gonna come, please let me come...!"

"Let go, sweet girl. You've done so well for me. Let go, and let me take care of you." Soren wraps both his arms around my shoulders and torso now, leaning over me and fucking me fast and rough like a beast.

We are in the stables, after all.

The sheer intensity of Soren's thrusts bring me to the edge, and his praise sends me over, shuddering and crying and thrashing against his grip. He doesn't let up the pace, even speeding up if at all possible. His thrusts draw out my orgasm and send me hurtling toward another. His cock, his spanks, his finger swirling tight circles around my needy clit -- it's too much, and as I sob and break apart in his arms, he holds himself deep and fills me up at last.

We collapse to the floor together, my tired, sweaty body pressed against his. Cali shuffles and stares down at us, but I'm too far gone to care. Soren presses kiss after kiss into my forehead, my cheeks, my lips, my eyelids. He massages my sore muscles and speaks soft, soothing words.

"I'll take care of you, Lara. I will always take care of you and give you everything that you need. Everything that you want. You'll learn our ways and our customs, and in return, you'll have a more devoted mate than you could ever ask for."

"Thank you...Soren." I curl up against him, so small under his massive body, and listen to his heart beat. We may be on an alien world, but the beat of his heart is as strong and vital as ever. I'm too tired, too overwhelmed to speak, so I close my eyes and let my body do the talking.

WONDERMENT

SOREN

After my mate and I recover and clean ourselves, I pull her up onto Cali and we set off. I let her choose the place, so we're going to go see all of the things she pointed out from the windows back at the cottage.

I'm excited to show and tell her more about my planet. My heart leaps in my chest every time she gasps in wonderment. The ruddy flush of her cheeks and the way she points out everything we pass doesn't get old. She seems genuinely interested in what I have to say.

Even after our little 'learning opportunity' back at the stables, she doesn't hold it against me. She knows it's for the best, and it's not like she didn't enjoy herself as well.

My lips curl up into a grin. The way she looked, sagging against me as I spanked her pretty little bottom again and again... My cock throbs just at the thought of it. But there will be plenty of time for that later. Right now, I want to show her just how vast and wondrous my world truly is.

Each couple signed up for the surrogacy program has their own cottage and plot of land. They say it's for the women's safety, but it's just as much for ours. I smell other males in the air, but they're far off now.

No one to steal away my sweet Lara. I alone get to enjoy the swell of her curves and the taste between her thighs. Only I get to hear her sounds of pleasure and her cries of delight. I know that it won't always be like this, but for now, it's...nice.

We walk down a shaded trail toward a waterfall. Birds and butterflies flutter past us, painting the forest in shades of red, yellow, and green. It seems so normal, so natural to me, but to Lara this is like something out of a fairy tale. She will come to get used to it in time, but I'm going to enjoy every squeal of surprise while I can.

"This is so beautiful..." Lara sighs.

"It is, my sweet. And I promise, you will get to see it all."

The path opens up to a shallow pool and an overhanging rock formation. The rush of the waterfall drowns out all other noise, splashing down the rocks and into the pool below. Near the shore, brightly colored little fish zip back and forth. They use their huge tail fins to propel themselves out of the water in a dazzling display. "Oh my gosh!" Lara covers her mouth, watching them splash and jump over one another. It's like the most intricate fountain show, but with live fish instead. I knew she'd love it. "They're so cute!"

And that's only one stop on our tour.

She leans back against me as we ride. I know she doesn't realize, but the swell of her ass and the sweet, soft scent of her so close has me hanging on by a thread. It's not the alpha rut anymore that seized me with such fierce abandon, but something deeper. It sits at the very core of my being, an omnipresent partner.

A friend.

That's when it hits me. The feelings that poured out of me the first time we mated weren't just a surge of hormones driving me to spill into the nearest female. It was more than that, and it stayed with me to this day.

Lara is my heartmate. She has to be. My one and only. My star amidst a moonless night.

She nestles in closer to me, oblivious to my thoughts. When I signed the contract for the ISA, I didn't know what to expect. A willing vessel for my child. That was it. That was the bare minimum, and that's all they promised.

But Lara...

She's so much more than that. She's soft, and kind, and beautiful...

She makes me want to shout to the stars how much I love her. And all at the same time, she makes me want to hide her away from the world and keep her to myself forever.

It's in this moment of blissful, radiant revelation that I know she's the one for me. Already I can see her amidst our people, a babe on her breast and another in her belly. I can already tell she will be a wonderful mother. I hear the emotion in her voice when she talks about her family. About her life on Earth.

And that's precisely the reason that I'll never be able to truly have her. She likely doesn't feel the same, and even if she did, a contract is a contract.

Lara came here to lay with me, a total stranger, in exchange for food and resources. That was it. The circumstances were dire down on Earth, and I could provide everything she ever needed and more here on my planet.

But it wasn't that simple. With the same conviction that told me she was my fated one, I held another, secret fear in my heart.

That if she had to choose between me and her family down on Earth, she would leave, and I would never see her again.

POSITIVE PREGNANCY TEST

LARA

The exploration -- not to mention our little 'detour' -- takes nearly all day. By the time we arrive back at the cottage, the pale moon hangs high in the sky and I'm struggling to stay awake.

My stomach feels a bit queasy, but I haven't eaten for most of the day. Soren, of course, insists I eat something. There's nothing I'd rather do than crawl into bed, but I humor him. I take the tablet and order up a strawberry milkshake and a slice of cake to end the day.

He doesn't comment on my choice of meal -- he said he could have whatever I wanted, after all -- but when I take the first bite of cake, my stomach twists in on itself.

The food hurtles right back up the way it came and I cover my mouth, eyes wide, as I rush to the bathroom. "My sweet?" I hear him call from behind me. "Are you all right?"

The door bangs open on its hinges and I barely make it to the toilet in time before I'm doubled over, retching the day's contents into the bowl. I heave and gag, bracing myself on the porcelain until there's nothing left. Soren stays by my side, gently brushing my hair out of my face and rubbing warm circles on my back.

When I'm finished, my whole body shakes and I feel like I can barely stand. Soren wraps his arms around me. "Do you feel ill? Do you need me to call the doctor?"

If I didn't feel so horrible, it would almost be cute how doting he's become. I brush him away and try to catch my breath. "I'm fine...just need..."

"What do you need? Anything you want, you got it." Soren runs a nervous hand through his hair. "I'm sorry I made you eat, I thought it would help with the cramps, but..."

"Not your fault," I croak. I try to get to my feet, but the world still spins too much for that. Cold tile floor it is. "Just bring me some water. And some crackers, if you can?"

"Of course." He kisses the top of my head and hurries off, leaving me with some much-needed silence. I let out one shaky breath, then another. All right. Don't panic.

They told us this would happen. The nurses when they came for their checkups said to be on the lookout for this sort of thing. My stomach cramps again, but nothing comes up. I press a hand to the sensitive area. Does this mean...?

Heart pounding in my chest, I open the cabinet under the sink and start filing through the various items. Bandages, no. Painkillers, no. Cotton swabs, still no. At last I find the box I'm looking for, all the way at the back. My hands shake as I open the package.

A pregnancy test.

Despite the alien nature of everything else on this planet, the pregnancy tests are the same ones I remember from Earth. It makes sense, though. Why would an alien pregnancy test work on a human?

I stare at the small stick in front of me. In the next few moments, whatever happens could change the course of my trip -- and my life -- forever. I think back on all the time I've spent with Soren. All the incredible sex and all the breathtaking views on this amazing planet. All in the name of duty, right?

I chuckle. It stopped being a 'duty' long ago. My hand rests against my belly and I wobble to my feet to sit over the toilet seat.

So, this was it. Of course the nurses would confirm it at my next appointment, but if it came out positive and I actually was pregnant...

A chill raced up my spine and mental images flooded my brain. A soft, squealing baby nestled in my arms. Soren standing next to me in a warm embrace. Would the baby be alien like him? Or human like me?

They'd said our DNA was compatible, but as for what we'd create together...

Would the child be a halfling of both worlds? And would they be able to live and thrive in this new environment? My heart squeezes as I remember Janie and Iris. At how hard Janie worked to provide for her little girl. Now I will have a chance to bring new life into the world -- this world -- and for all the excitement, I'm nervous, too.

I bite my lip and shove the stick between my legs, letting the stream catch the absorbent tip. I know in my gut, but I don't dare to believe it. I need proof. And the proof is right here, on this little plastic stick.

Popping on the cap, I set it on the edge of the sink and close my eyes. Any second now. Any second...

Finally, I can't wait anymore. I have to know. Or rather, I have to confirm what I already feel in my heart.

In shaking hands, I grab the test and check the result window. There it is, clear as day.

Pregnant.

I'm not prepared for the rush of emotions that come next. Excitement. Relief. Anticipation. Nervousness. And on top of all of them, louder than the rest -- love. Pure, sweet love for the life we've created. My hand cradles my belly, and tears spring to my eyes.

I did it. No. We did it.

And the best gift of all, besides the fact that I have a little one on the way?

They're not going to send me home. I get to stay here, on Aesir, with Soren.

At least...until the year is up. And then?

My heart clenches at the thought, but I did sign a contract...

Soren knocks on the door, knocking me out of my thoughts. "Lara? You okay in there? I brought the water and crackers. Can you get up? Do I need to come in?"

"No!" I say a little too quickly. "I'm fine, I'll...I'll be right out!"

After a few seconds to compose myself, I gather the stick and the paperwork and push open the door. Soren's already standing there with a worried look on his face. "Darling, are you..."

I cut him off and throw myself into his embrace. The warmth of his touch and the quickness of his heart give me the courage for what I do next. I pull away, smile as big as I can, and push the stick into his hand. "Look."

He turns over the stick, laughably small in his huge hands. "This is one of your...human supplies?" He cocks an eyebrow, shaking it next to his ear like it's supposed to make a noise. "What is it?"

I choke out a laugh at his reaction. He might be a fearsome warlord on his planet, but right now, he's my adorably clueless mate. "It's a pregnancy test, Soren. See there?" I take the test from him and point at the window. "That means I'm pregnant. I'm carrying your baby."

The words slowly register in his head, and when they do he knocks the test out of my hand and pulls me into a fierce embrace. "We did it?" He says incredulously. "We made a baby?"

I pull away just enough to look him in the eyes. His golden lips fall open, his ever-serious eyes laced with tears. I cup his cheek and he covers my hand with his own, pressing a kiss to the back of my wrist. "We did it, Soren. Together." Hope and excitement and love, love, love pours out of me and fills the room. "You're going to be a father."

He lets out a loud, hearty laugh before peppering me with kisses all over my face, neck and shoulders. "This is amazing!" He touches and caresses anywhere he can reach but lingers on my belly. "You're amazing, Lara."

"Hey," I say with a wink. "Couldn't have done it without you."

Pressed up against him like this, I can feel his cock throb at my words. To think that I can carry a child for a man like him...it still seems like a dream. These last few weeks have been nothing but sheer delight, and now that I'm with child, I'm sure he'll only get more doting and protective.

Which, to my secret shame, I find kinda hot.

Still glowing from the praise, I point to the paperwork discarded on the floor next to the test. "They said we need to call them as soon as we know, so they can get everything checked out --"

"Well then what are we waiting for?" Soren scoops me up in his arms like he did that first day, heading for the door. "Let's go right now."

"Now?" I'm still in my pajamas, but he kisses me and tells me I look beautiful anyway. All I can do is laugh, because he's not taking no for an answer. Instead I curl into his protective embrace and daydream about the future.

A future with Soren. Myself. And our child.

COMMS PANEL

LARA

TWO MONTHS LATER

"I'm not crippled. Just pregnant!"

Ever since I threw up that first night, Soren's protective instincts are on overdrive. Not that they weren't before, but the addition of a new life on the way has turned him into a possessive father-to-be.

It's a bit stifling in some ways to have him fussing over me, but I would be lying if I said I didn't kinda like it. For nineteen years I put others first and remained in the background. After my parents died, I spent so much time trying to figure out how to get Janie and Iris what they needed. Now, having Soren treat me like the only woman on the planet is a nice change of pace.

Two months pass in a blur of doctor's appointments, cravings, and morning sickness. Thankfully that part seems to be dying down. I realized why Soren was so upset about it the first time -- his race doesn't get morning sickness. Their constitution is also a lot stronger than ours, so if one of them started puking, it was very severe indeed.

No wonder he panicked.

As our baby develops, I can tell that Soren's getting more and more excited. So am I, to be honest. He's always gone out of his way to make me feel comfortable and safe, and he's gone above and beyond even that these days. I don't want for anything, I get to eat whatever I want, the lands surrounding our cottage are filled with natural beauty, and Soren brings me to climax after climax in bed. This is practically paradise...

But today, when Soren presents me with my first pair of maternity clothes, I feel a pang of guilt. And not only that. Of homesickness.

Blame it on the hormones, but when Soren gifts me the clothes and I end up bursting into ugly tears in the bedroom, he takes it personally. "Darling, why are you crying? Are the clothes not to your liking? I can have them exchanged--"

"No," I sniff. "They're beautiful. It's just." I hug my knees to my chest and let out a sigh. "I miss my sister. She never had an opportunity like this. She got pregnant as a teen and then my parents died and we barely had enough to keep our heads above water. Then the food shortage hit, and..." I can't bring myself to finish the sentence.

Soren doesn't say anything at first. He watches me with careful, intent eyes, then joins me on the bed.

Strong, warm arms wrap me in his soothing embrace. It doesn't solve everything, but his presence makes me feel a little lighter. I bury my face into his shirt. It's one of his nicer uniforms and here I am getting tears and snot on it, but he doesn't seem to mind.

When I catch my breath, I look up at him with wide, teary eyes. "Is there any way I can talk to her? Do the...signals work that far away? Can I call her?"

Even at the thought of hearing her voice, my chest seizes again and I let out another sob. How was she? How was Iris? Were they okay? Did they get the payments?

Here I was having the time of my life on Aesir, and they were still stuck on Earth. It didn't seem fair.

"I'm not sure," Soren admits. "Let me check the comms panel."

He gets up and inspects the tablet-like object next to the doorway in each room. I can barely see what he's doing, only that there's a lot of typing. The lights flicker for a fraction of a second and then go dim, leaving us in the darkness.

I gasp and pull the pillow close to my chest. "Soren? What happened?"

"Just a moment, sweet. Working as intended!"

Not even a second after he says that, the lights come back on and the systems beep online once more. A female voice comes from the speaker on the wall. "Off-world communications unlocked."

My mouth drops open. "How did you..."

Soren beams with pride. "I had to override the power distribution grid to boost the signal, but..." He rubs the back of his neck. "Worth it?"

"Worth it?" I crow. "Oh my gosh, this is amazing! Does this mean I can talk to her now?"

Soren nods. "We can't sustain these power levels for long -- that's why the power went out for a minute -- but it should be enough for you to contact your loved ones."

I wipe the tears from my eyes and jump up to give him a giant hug. He chuckles softly. "Remember what I told you, Lara?" He hums next to my ear. "I will do anything for you. Anything."

"Thank you," I whisper. "How do I..."

"I've got the interface pulled up," Soren points out. "Just type in her number and you should be good to go. One more thing, though: see that timer? You only have that much time before the systems reboot, but that's the best I could do." He stares at his feet. "I hope it's enough."

"It is!" I cry. "Thank you. Again." Honestly, it's more than enough. What kind of man re-routes the entire power grid just so I can talk to my sister back home? This one, apparently.

Aesir men are something else.

He heads for the doorway, then stops. "I have to go out today to oversee some matters with my own people. I will not be long, however, and shall return by sunset. Will you be alright until then?"

I nod. I haven't had a day to myself in weeks, and as great as Soren's company is, it will be nice to just relax. "I'll be fine. Don't worry."

He snickers. "I'm your alpha. It's my job to worry. See you tonight." With a final peck on the cheek, he leaves.

THE ROOM FALLS into silence and I get up to investigate the comms panel. Sure enough, a timer at the corner of the screen ticks down. If I'm going to call Janie, I need to do it now. So with a deep breath, I tap in her number on the screen, put the call up on the monitor, and crawl into bed.

It rings for what feels like forever. I didn't even think to check what time it might be on Earth. I hope she's still awake and that I'm not bothering her. Just when I think she's not going to pick up, the panel makes a click-beep and a familiar voice echoes through the room.

"Lara, is that you?"

Those four simple words pack such an emotional punch I nearly burst into tears all over again. "Yeah," I croak. "It's me."

For a moment neither of us talk. We can't even see each other and the signal is still weak, but I needed this more than I realized.

"Hey, sis." Janie says. Her voice cracks, and I can't tell if it's from the static on the call or her emotion. I'm tearing up as well, so probably a bit of both.

"How are you doing? Is Iris there?" I can't wait any longer. I have to know.

"Yes, she's right here. Say hi to Auntie Lara!"

I hear the shuffling sounds of movement. "Ann...tee..."

And there she is. I choke back a sob. She's the one I'm doing all this for.

"Hey there," I coo. "Are you being a good girl for your mommy? I miss you."

"She's a handful as always, but things are a lot better than they were."

"So, I take it they came through? You got the stuff?" I fiddle with the buttons on my dress and try to hold it together. "I was so worried about you."

"It came just in the nick of time, just like they said it would." Janie pauses. "I don't know what we would have done if you hadn't..." She stops. Clears her throat. "But how about you? Are they treating you all right? Cause if they're not, I'm not above hopping on a spaceship to come kick some alien butt."

We both share a laugh, and for a second its almost like old times. I lean back into the pillows and stare up at the skylight and the unfamiliar stars.

"I started taking some online classes, you know." Janie's voice sounds a little more relaxed now. Like she's just as happy to hear from me as well. "With the stipend from the ISA I don't have to worry about putting food on the table so I can study while Iris is sleeping. If I keep it up, I'll be able to land a better job for us."

"That's great," I say, and I mean it. I'm beyond overjoyed that Janie's finally taking steps to further her education. She had to drop out of school to take care of Iris, and then when our parents died she never had a chance to go back. My heart warms at the thought. Maybe she'll finally have a chance to pursue her dream, and it's all thanks to me.

Or rather, all thanks to this planet and their hunky warlords.

"I'm well," I say, placing a hand over my stomach. "Really well, actually. The alien I matched with...well..." I know she can't see me, but a blush colors my cheeks and ears anyway. "He's quite the lover, if you know what I mean."

"Oooh, spicy. You'll have to tell me all the dirty details when you get home."

Right. Home. The thought clenches in my gut. I know I've gotta leave when the year's up, but the longer I stay here, the harder and harder I fall for my golden alien warlord.

Yeah. Like that. MY alien? We're just in a contract together, chemically bonded by hormones like two lab rats breeding in a cage. This isn't real. Can't be. I have to remind myself of that.

Too bad my heart isn't listening.

"Lara? You still there?" Janie's voice jerks me out of my thoughts.

"Oh, yeah. I am. Sorry. Got lost in thought for a moment there." I run a hand through my hair and let out a sigh. My heart pounds with thoughts of Soren. And more than that -- thoughts of our child.

Could I really leave my own baby behind?

"I might not be up there, but I can still tell when something's on your mind. Spit it out."

I wince. Damn, she's good. "I...I think I'm starting to fall for Soren."

There's a long silence, and already I'm cursing myself for saying anything. I know it's a stupid idea, but now that I've said it, it feels so much more real...

"Are you sure?" Janie says at last. "That's...a lot."

"Tell me about it." I groan. "Am I totally screwed?"

Another pause. "You want the truth, or...?"

I flash back to the moment I realized I was pregnant. I would have to tell her sooner or later. "Janie, I --"

And with that, the call ends with a robotic beep.

Connection limit exceeded. Rerouting power sources...

I sit there in the darkness, the words still stuck on my tongue.

MOTHER'S RING

SOREN

It feels good to stretch my legs again. To feel the rush of blood and battle. My months with Lara have been nothing short of exquisite, but I still have responsibilities to my people.

It's the first time returning to my village since meeting Lara, and everyone seems to want something. Our planet is now at peace, yes, but there are still petty squabbles among the villagers that need mediation. Apparently a gang of bandits thought they could pull a fast one and strike while I wasn't around.

That was their first mistake...and their last.

My men and I hunted them down, and it almost unnerved me how much I relished eliminating the threat. It reminded me of the old days. Of the war.

But I don't want to think about that. Now we have peace...and I have Lara.

I idly wonder how she's doing as I head with my men to the tavern. We're celebrating a job well done, and it's also a convenient place to talk to everyone at one time. I can't wait to tell them what I've discovered, but a small part of me still shies away.

Funny, isn't it? That a revered warlord could shy away from anything.

When it comes to Lara, all bets are off.

I greet each of my men in turn, buying us all a round of drinks before we settle into our chairs in a well-worn corner of the tavern. Just like old times, indeed.

My oldest friend and right hand man Kyvan raises a glass. "To Soren! May we enjoy many more centuries of Aesir's peace!"

The others echo the toast and toast back, clinking their glasses together. I let out a sigh as I take a long drink and savor the taste. "It's good to be home."

A brief silence settles and I sense each of my men gauging me. They all want to ask me about Lara and about the ISA. It seemed like such an outlandish idea at first -- even dangerous. Some of them even warned me not to do it, but once they hear about my results I have no doubt they'll be rushing to the office to sign up themselves.

"I'm sure you all have questions," I say, trying to keep the pensive thoughts at bay. "But the truth is, I don't even know where to begin."

"Don't keep us in suspense, Soren," Kyvan prompts. "Tell us about the girl. You knocked her up yet?"

A streak of possessiveness flares up, but it's only Kyvan. If he knew what I know, he wouldn't use such crass words. A sense of pride fills me up in its place, and the sweet memory of her smile greets me every time I close my eyes. I clear my throat. "She is with child, yes."

A hearty series of cheers and hollers go up. I let them have their fun, and when the noise dies down I look at each of them, my face serious. These are men I've battled with to the edge of the galaxy and beyond. We had held each other's lives in our hands more times than I could count. They were like brothers to me, and now I was about to share one of my most personal secrets.

"There's more," I start. I stare into my mug and try to think of the words. "I think she's..." I gulp down the last of the liquid and pray that it gives me courage. "I think she's my heart-mate."

The raucous cheers die in an instant. Nothing but stone-cold silence fills the air between us. They know the gravity of this confession as well as I do, and it takes a few moments for them to process.

Kyvan speaks up first. "Are you certain?"

I think for a moment, but the answer's already embedded in my heart. "Yes. She's the one. I know it."

The men sit back in their chairs, watching me with wide-eyed admiration. "Whoa," one of the other men says. "That's huge. And a human, at that..."

I shake my head. I know how ridiculous this all sounds, but I can't deny the way that I feel. "It surprises me just as much, I assure you. When I signed the contract I expected nothing more than a willing human for our little...transaction. What I got was..." My voice deepens, cock twitching in my trousers. "So much more."

Kyvan claps me on the shoulder. "Well, I'm happy for you, man. But what does that mean for the contract? She's supposed to go back at some point, right?"

My fists clench at the thought. My nails dig into my palms as my heart thuds harder in my chest. No. I can't lose her. I can't let her leave. She's mine. My heart-mate.

The very floor rumbles with the strength of my emotion. I shoot up from my chair. It clatters backward. My men stare at me, but I don't care. I can't do this right now. "I told you. She's mine." That's the only answer I have at the moment, and the only answer they'll get.

For now, I need a moment alone.

I stomp out of the tavern and into the stormy night. The weather matches my mood -- foul and raging with the very fury of nature itself.

I should have known better. I should have held myself back, done something, anything, to avoid imprinting on her like this.

But it's already done, and now I can't imagine life without her.

No one understands. Not my men. Not the ISA. Hell, probably not even Lara herself. This isn't some passing fancy. I don't just want her around. I need her.

Does she not know how rare a heart-mate is? How sacred?

Those words would mean nothing to her, but everything to me. A heart-mate was the greatest connection two people could ever have. Our destinies were literally written in the stars, fated to come together since the day we were born. She's the missing piece I longed for all these years, and she doesn't even know it yet. How could I ever let her go?

I want to say screw the contract, screw the ISA and screw the entire planet if they were to stand against us. I would pay for her sister and niece out of my own pocket for the rest of their lives if it meant I could have more time with Lara. I would fight anyone who tried to tell me otherwise.

I growl and stalk across the village to my dwelling. Busting open the door, I make a beeline for the bedroom and throw open the trunk at the foot of my bed.

There, kept safe ever since I reached manhood, is a small black box. My mother, before she passed on, told me to open it once I found someone worth fighting for.

I was young, brash, and stupid back then. I cared only about proving myself in battle and had no idea what she was talking about. Now, as I hold her parting gift in my hands, I finally know what she meant.

We don't fight simply for the sake of it. I put my all into defending my home and my people because it was the right thing to do, yes. But now I realize what it's all for. To keep her safe. To raise our child. To pass on my legacy.

I crack open the lid to the box and there it is. An intricate silver ring inlaid with a single moonstone. Ancient runes encircle the band with our family's creed. The ring hangs heavy in my palm, but it's not because of the metal. The sheer emotional weight of it washes over me as I think back to my younger years. This is the very same ring my mother wore during her mating ceremony.

The same she gave to me to pass on to my chosen one, when the time came.

It's perfect.

Turning it over in my hands, I feel the same electric pull in my chest that I did when I first met her. She's the one. There's no doubt about it. And even though this ring is too large for her delicate fingers, I can easily have it resized.

If I have any chance of getting Lara to stay, I need to do this right. I'll wrap things up here and I'll return to her as soon as I can.

Before the baby comes and before she's whisked away back to Earth, I'm going to ask her to be my wife. To stay with me and raise our child.

Forever.

PROPOSAL

LARA

"Soren? What's this all about?" I giggle as he leads me by the hand toward an unknown location. He simply said he had a surprise for me, then he put on a blindfold and carried me over to Cali. We rode for probably half an hour, and now he led me on foot. Just what was going on? And why all the secrecy?

No matter how much I poke him, he won't tell me a thing. Which was both exciting and nerve-wracking, to be honest. For all I knew, he could have been leading me to my doom.

But I knew him better than that now. Soren, for his outwardly brusque exterior, treasured me more than anyone ever had. He did his best to provide for my every need and want. He went above and beyond, like that time he rerouted the power to let me call my sister.

So why did the stirring in my heart feel suspiciously like love?

I think again about my conversation with Janie. She knew just how tough it could be to sleep with someone and have them abandon you. Soren wouldn't do that -- not by choice -- but it's not like he has a choice in the first place.

The contract still binds us in black and white, saying that my time on this planet could not exceed one year. There's no intention to house and provide for me, nor for my sister and niece, for longer than the required period to bear their next generation.

"Okay." Soren's hand at my back and his warm voice brings me back, but a fresh pain still simmers in my heart. No matter how much I care for him, I can't stay. I have a life on Earth. I have a family that needs me.

"We're here," Soren says, and he slips off my blindfold.

I suck in a gasp, and each reservation I have shatters like glass.

It's beautiful.

I don't know how he's done it, but before me is a lovingly recreated vintage drive-in movie theater. A tall screen sits upright on the green surrounded with speakers and twinkling lights. Bursts of colorful flowers surround us and in the center lies a huge checkered blanket and a wicker basket.

"You didn't..." I put a hand over my mouth in shock. My mind reels. All the late night conversations we had. All the little things we discussed here and there. He remembered them all.

Too many emotions hit me all at once. Gratitude. Excitement. Awe. And there's no use denying it any longer -- love.

Soren takes my hand and leads me across the green to the picnic blanket. "What do you think?" He says quietly. His voice is lower. More serious, somehow. "I know you have been missing Earth, so...I thought I would give you a taste of home."

"How did you do this?" I ask, looking around. "I mean, this is amazing!"

He shrugs. "I had some favors to call in. I wanted to give you a night you would never forget."

I melt a little bit inside. "You've already been so good to me. Why all of this? You didn't have to..."

"I know." He pauses, and that same serious tone is still in his voice. "But I wanted to. I...care about you, Lara. A lot. You make me feel things I've never felt before."

My heart skips a beat. "What are you saying?" My pulse thuds in my ears. I take in the chirping of the birds nearby. The fresh breeze. The soft lights hanging from the trees, and the sun just starting to droop past the horizon.

"You have to understand..." He starts, jaw working over the words. "This is uncharted territory for me. I've been across the galaxy and have faced some of the meanest, toughest opponents in existence." Soren swallows. "Yet this trumps them all."

I lean forward and clasp his hand in my own. It trembles, only slightly. "Is something wrong?"

"No, not that." He lets out a nervous chuckle. "Nothing like that. It's just...when I signed the contract, I didn't expect anything like this to happen." He looks up, meets my eyes. "I'm willing to bet you didn't either."

He got me there. "I didn't know what to expect," I say honestly. "You have to realize how scared I was, how desperate..." A lump forms in my throat and I swallow it back down. Tears prick at the corners of my eyes.

"I did what I had to do."

Soren draws closer. His lips brush my ear and send a chill down my spine. "And now?"

I somehow remember to breathe. I turn my head ever so slightly until we're face to face. We're so different. Two different cultures. Two different planets. But when I look into his deep, dark eyes, I feel like I belong for the first time in my life. "Now...I can't think of anywhere I'd rather be."

"I'm glad," Soren rumbles. His heat pours over me and his body perfectly fits with mine. We are two pieces of a puzzle, and I want to remember this moment for the rest of my life. "And that's why I want to ask you something."

I pull back. My heart leaps into my throat. My lips part in a silent question. "What...?"

"Close your eyes one more time," he whispers.

As the world fades into blackness, he moves away from me and I hear a short rustle.

"Open them."

I do, and he's there on one knee. Just like in the movies.

My mouth drops open.

"Lara. You have changed the way I look at the world. I thought I had it all, but I didn't realize how much I was missing until the day I met you. I know I'm not supposed to care about you like this, but I do. I can't help it. I can't control it. And I don't want to anymore." He pulls out a small box and holds it out to me. Even through the blur of my tears, I can see the sparkle of a silver ring and a beautiful pale stone.

"This was my mother's," he says reverently. "She gave it to me to pass on one day. And that day has finally come." His eyes sparkle with affection and unbridled emotion. "I would battle the galaxy all over again just to keep you at my side. Will you do me the honor of becoming my wife?"

My breath catches in my throat and the world -- no, the universe -- narrows to just the two of us. Only now do I grasp the enormity of all that he's done. Crafting the replica drive in movie theater. Offering me his mother's ring. And most of all, going against not only the ISA but Aesir customs by asking me to be his wife.

I take in a ragged, shuddering breath and blink away the tears. What would Janie think? Would I ever see Earth again? Would I ever see Iris again? There are too many questions to consider. Too many warring thoughts and feelings and values. But despite it all, there's only one answer on my mind.

"Yes," I whisper. "Yes, Soren. I would love to be your wife."

It doesn't matter what trials we have to face in the future. For this brilliant, shining moment, there's just us. He is mine and I am his. I can put everything out of my mind and focus on our bond. The little one growing inside me.

And come what may, we'll face it together.

Soren pops up from his knee and takes me into his arms. His grip turns almost crushing. His lips crash against mine and the passion behind his movements is rivaled only by the first time we met -- that hazy, heat-fueled incident when we were still strangers.

But we are strangers no more, and I want to give him everything I have. Everything I am. Not because a contract made me do it. Not because my hormones made me do it. Because I love him, and he loves me.

It takes a moment for me to register anything outside ourselves, but I hear it again. A voice, strangely familiar...

"Lara, I need to speak with you. Urgently."

Thoughts still hazy, I tear myself away from Soren and turn toward the source of the noise. He holds me possessively, the ring still in his hand and pressing against mine. But what I see waiting there is nothing I could have expected.

It's Orvox, and her normally professional demeanor has cracked into something bordering on panic. My stomach drops at the sight. It was in the rules, they were not to interrupt us except in case of emergency, and...

Oh my god, what had happened?

"Orvox?" I croak. "What's going on?"

Her face darkens. "There's been an accident. On Earth. You need to come with me."

And just like that, the fleeting happiness dashes upon the jagged rocks of reality.

"W-what are you talking about? What happened? Is Iris okay? Is Janie?"

She presses her already-thin lips together even tighter. "A riot broke out near your sister's home and she was injured. She's alive and stable, and she has been transported to the hospital. But you have a right to know. Your sister begged the doctors to contact you. To come back and help out in case..." Orvox licks her lips. "In case something happens. You'll need to take care of the child, Iris."

Suddenly, my fairy tale romance felt so silly. So selfish. I came up here in the first place to protect them, and if I couldn't even do that...

Soren tightens his grip against me, and even I can feel his barely-leashed control fraying. "You should let me go. Let me take care of them. Those who hurt your kin will not live to see the morning." His voice, a marked change from his honeyed words just moments earlier, is pure fury now. "Give me leave and I will avenge them, Lara. This I swear to you."

My heart's racing and the tears are pouring and everything's moving fast, much too fast. What did she mean, an accident? And what did she mean, 'if something happens?'

Flashbacks to losing my parents take hold and I start shaking, breaths coming in panicked tearful gasps. This can't be happening. Not again. Not after everything Janie and I went through together. Not her too.

Not her too.

I turn to Soren, and even though his warrior's protectiveness warms my heart, I know I have to do this alone. "Soren..." I reach up and cradle his cheek with my hand. "...I can't stay here, I have to go to her..." My heart shatters further with every word, but there's nothing else I can do.

From the highest high to the lowest low, all in a matter of seconds. But I knew in my heart of hearts what I had to do. Janie needed me. Iris needed me.

Soren pulls me into another fierce kiss, holding me so tight I can practically feel my bones creaking. "I will wait for you, my Lara. If that is your wish. I..." His face, still mottled with fury and concern, softens ever so slightly. "I love you. And I will continue to love you, no matter what choice you make. You are what's important to me now." He takes my hand with a tenderness I'll never forget and slips the ring onto my finger. Leaning his forehead against mine, he rubs small circles on my back while whispering soft, comforting words in my ears.

"I will be here, my Lara. My starlight. Go to your sister. See that she is well. I shall not forget you."

It's the hardest decision I've ever made in my life. Harder than deciding to sign the contract. Harder than working back-breaking hours just to put food on the table for Janie and Iris. But in the end, I know what I have to do.

"I love you, Soren." And with that, I turn away from the love of my life -- from my new fiancé -- and prepare to leave the planet.

HOPELESSNESS

SOREN

I thought I knew pain when I faced certain death at the hands of an intergalactic dictator. I thought I knew hopelessness when I saw my men fall one by one with nothing I could do to stop it.

I was wrong.

The pain that runs through me when I see my heart-mate walking away from me, possibly forever, tears at my very soul. Anger and guilt and fear flood through me in equal measure, but there's nothing I can do.

I have to let her -- and the ISA -- handle this.

And I've never felt so powerless in all my life.

She turns and looks back at me, and for a moment I see the weight of her decision on her face. She wants to stay. I know she does. But she can't.

I raise my hand to my lips and blow her a kiss, trying to put all the love I have into that simple action. She returns the gesture and disappears into the transport with Orvox. Soon, they're both out of sight.

I'm alone.

There's no one out here. I picked a remote area that would be just for us, so that we wouldn't be disturbed while I laid my own heart bare for the woman I hoped would be mine for the rest of our lives. The carefully constructed scene looks back at me, a mocking reminder of what almost was. The food sits untouched in the picnic basket. The champagne, uncorked.

Even the movie sits paused at the title screen, ready for us to share the night together.

But everything changed in that pivotal instant, and now I don't get to anymore.

With a snarl, I gather everything up as fast as I can. I don't want to see it. I don't want to be reminded of how hard I worked for her. Of how much I put on the line just to tell her that I loved her.

I know it's not her fault -- but that doesn't make it any easier. Every time I breathe, every time I close my eyes, I see her broken face. Her tears. And all at the same time, I see her smile. Her love. The joy we shared -- and the little one still forming in her belly.

That one socks me right in the gut. Our baby. Will Lara be alright without the Aesir nurses to monitor her pregnancy? I'm told that it's different than an Earth pregnancy, though I don't know by how much.

And what's more...will our baby be okay? Will I ever see them? Hold them in my arms?

So much is uncertain now, and I hate it. My scowl deepens. There were contingency sections in the contract for the case of emergencies, but I was so excited at the time that I tried not to think about the what ifs.

Now I have to.

With a sigh, I return to Cali and stroke her mane, trying to think of anything but my Earth-bound mate. She huffs and nudges at my shoulder, then looks this way and that. She knows something is up. Of course she does. We've worked together for so long that we understand each other.

"I'm sorry, girl," I say as I focus on her soft coat. "She's not coming back with us this time."

Cali stomps a hoof in protest.

"I know, I know. I'm not happy about it either. But she has to go help her family. You understand that right, girl? Family?"

Her nostrils flare and she lowers her head in agreement.

I climb up onto her back and start to lead her back toward the cottage, but I freeze. There's nothing left there for me but memories and pain. She might be gathering her things there right now, preparing to leave the planet. And if I see her again, I don't think I'll be able to stop myself from begging her to stay.

No. I have to do this. I have to be strong, for her.

So I turn Cali around and we start the long journey back to my home.

* * *

THE SILENT NIGHT and the long trek provides plenty of time to sit with my thoughts. Not that that's a good thing. I wonder how I'm going to tell my men. I wonder how I'm going to sleep at night without her next to me.

At least I hadn't introduced her to my clan yet. They would not miss her as much as I would. Of course, no one could miss her as much as I did right now. It's like a piece of me left with her, and without it I feel as empty as a black hole in space.

If there's one thing I've learned about Lara in the short time we spent together, it's how determined she is when she puts her mind to something. It is one of the first things I grew to love about her, besides her heavenly appearance of course. Not many women would have willingly offered themselves as surrogates to an unknown alien. But the fact that she did, and what's more, the reasons she did, speaks volumes about her character.

She would be a great wife and a great leader. If she chooses to come back.

My chest clenches again at the thought. I know we're heart-mates. I can feel it, deep down in her soul. Even though Lara grows further and further away, I still feel a part of her with me. Like the faintest heartbeat in the back of my mind. No matter what happens, no matter how far she goes, part of me will always be able to feel her there.

I'm told that true heart-mates, after their mating ceremony, can even share thoughts and feelings. I hope I get the chance to find out.

The sight of my mother's ring on her finger gives me hope. She will be back. I saw the love in her eyes. I saw the pain and the conflict when she had to leave.

All I have to do is wait. And somehow not go insane in the meantime.

* * *

WE'RE JUST GETTING ready to cross out of the ISA designated zone when I spot a guard tower up ahead. I grumble to myself. Great, another lackey. No doubt they've heard the situation by now, so they should have no problem letting me leave. I pull up to the window and a uniformed representative steps out.

"Ah, there you are. I am very sorry to hear about the incident regarding Miss Lara. Please rest assured that you will be issued a replacement mate if necessary. Would you like me to contact other candidates on your behalf?"

"What?!" I roar, unable to stop myself. I grab the man by the neck and lift him up into the air so he's face to face with me. "You will do no such thing, and I'm going to pretend you didn't even suggest such treason." My voice shakes, my rage prickles all the way through my skin, and I know I'm a hair's breadth away from snapping his neck right here. "My Lara is not a pawn or a bargaining chip. She is my heart-mate, and mark my words, I will have her back."

The guard squeals and claws at my hand around his throat, legs kicking helplessly in the air. "P-please, Warlord Soren! I meant n-no offense!" He gags and chokes, his stupid golden face taking on a darker, redder shade. I let out a breath before placing him back on the ground against my better judgment.

"All right, all right! I get it. I will mark that in your file, apologies! There's just one last thing I need you to sign off on, then." He grabs a clipboard from the small office and thrusts it toward me.

This guard really wanted to risk his life today, didn't he?

With a sigh, I take the clipboard and read through the form. My blood chills in an instant.

It's a waiver to nullify the contract -- meaning that I'm no longer obligated to send food and money down to Earth.

Screw that.

I grab the clipboard in both hands and snap it in half with a growl. Tossing the pieces to the dust, I look up at the cowering guardsman with murder in my eyes. "Does that answer your question?"

"Um, yes sir! Sorry to bother you!"

"Damn right," I grumble, before digging my heels into Cali's flanks and picking up speed.

I need to get out of here. I need something to take my mind off of things. Off of her. Guess I'll do the same thing I always did before she came into the picture: find something to fight and let my fists do the talking.

JANIE'S HOSPITAL BED

LARA

Few things compare to the sheer bliss of holding a sleeping child. Especially one you haven't seen in far too long.

I hold a sleeping Iris on my chest while I sit next to Janie's hospital bed. She's also resting, and at last I have a moment of silence. Ever since I got the message that Janie was hurt, everything felt like a blur. A long, chaotic blur. And here I was, back on Earth with my sister and niece, like nothing ever happened.

Almost.

A few things were markedly different -- the rosy flush on Iris' cheeks, for one. Janie and Iris both looked more healthy and vibrant than I'd seen them in years. Even with Janie laid up with a broken leg, there's more color in her face than before. Her eyes are starting to carry that same zest for life that I grew up with. Little by little, they were both recovering, thanks to the food shipments and stipends from the ISA.

And it wasn't just the food, either -- Janie was going back to school online now, and was even able to afford advanced medical care for her leg. I shudder to think what might have happened otherwise...

I didn't realize just how much it would change our lives when I signed that contract and went up there.

Or how much it would change mine.

I place my free hand over my stomach, only barely starting to swell with child. I worry about carrying an alien pregnancy to term here on Earth, but doctors from the ISA are standing by in case I need anything.

There's one very important element I'm missing, though: Soren.

My heart aches for him every day that we're apart, but it wasn't really much of a choice, was it? I couldn't abandon my sister and niece. Not for the hottest, sweetest man (or alien) in the universe.

The sun sets and I lay Iris down in her small bed, then get up and stretch my legs. Walking across the room, I pull aside the curtains and stare out the hospital window, trying to catch a glimpse of the stars. I have no idea where he is, but looking up there makes me feel less alone. Like he can see me, somehow. Sense me.

I fiddle with the silver ring on my finger. It was the last thing he gave me before I had to leave. He'd asked me to marry him.

I'd said yes, hadn't I? Or did I get a chance to? It all happened so fast, and fears for Janie's safety soon took over any elation I may have had.

Slipping off the ring, I roll it around in my hand. Fine characters mark the inside of the ring in a language I can't understand. The translator doesn't work down here, and even if it did, I could only understand spoken voices. Not printed words.

I'll have to ask Soren what it means when I go back.

The thought comes without warning. I let out an involuntary gasp. *When I go back.* Was that even possible? When they off-boarded me, they gave me all kinds of paperwork and drugs to help readjust to Earth's atmosphere. It felt...weird, being back on Earth.

Familiar and unfamiliar all at the same time. And as I find myself staring up into space, my heart cries out where my voice cannot.

I miss him.

"Still looking for him?" Janie's voice startles me and I turn around to face her. She's awake, eyes half-lidded as she lays propped up on the inclined mattress.

"I -- " I try to retort, but it's no use. "How did you know?"

"I know my own sister. You miss him."

A lump forms in my throat. All I can do is nod. If I speak again, I don't know if I can hold back the tears.

"You didn't have to come all the way back, you know." Janie shifts to be further upright in bed. She takes a sip from the water bottle next to the bed and then checks the time. "I'll be fine."

I wince. "Come on, Janie. You and Iris...you're all I have left. I couldn't abandon you. Not like this."

Not like Iris' father, either.

There's more I want to say. So much more. But the words don't come. They stay lodged in my heart, covered up with so much grief that I can barely breathe. I sit down in the chair next to the bed again and stare out into the blackness, willing the stars to take my worries away.

"Are you feeling okay?" I ask after a time.

Janie nods. "I'm fine." She lets out a small laugh, then points to the cast on her leg. "Well, except for that. Puts a bit of a damper on things."

I smile in response. Even in the worst times, Janie always finds a way to make light of things. "Yeah, a bit."

"The doctors say you'll be good as new, though." I point out. "Lucky you were able to get to a hospital in time."

"Yeah," Janie says again, her eyes far away. "Lucky."

My stomach churns with an unasked question. Is it the same one she can't voice? I lick my lips, take a deep breath, and ask it.

"I...don't know what's going to happen with the contract." I fold my hands in my lap and look down, focusing on the ring. "I know you've been able to put money into savings, but..." I gesture at the hospital room. "All this isn't cheap, and..."

"Lara." She takes my hand. It's so soft and warm on my own, a contrast to the huge, coarse palms of the Aesir. "We've gotten through worse. We'll get through this too."

A single tear wells up at the corner of my eye. I sniff. "I know."

Because -- as usual -- we have no other choice.

A few more moments of silence pass between us, and I turn my attention to Iris' small, sleeping form. Her chest rises and falls slowly, her mouth slightly open. My heart aches in a whole different way when I see her now. Before, it was because she was my sister's child and had taken up residence in my heart as well. But now, there's another reason, too.

The alien baby growing inside me. I gently place a hand over my stomach and let my thoughts drift. If the contact was null and void by me leaving, what did that mean for the baby? What did that mean for us? I had too many questions, and not enough answers.

All I know is that meeting Soren -- and getting the help we needed from the ISA -- changed both of our lives. For good or for ill, things would never be the same.

"When you decided to leave," Janie pipes up. "What did he say?"

Her eyes are wistful, far away. Her hands bunch into the sheets.

"Who, Soren?" Even saying his name sends a chill down my spine. "What do you mean?"

"When you told him you had to leave," Janie continues. "What happened? How did he react?"

My face softens when I put two and two together. Iris' father had up and abandoned Janie the moment he found out she was pregnant. We never heard from him again. And now, seeing Janie's tear-streaked face, I know what she's really asking.

"He..." I start, trying to find the words as I go. But as the tearful scene plays out in my mind, it's more raw and vivid than any dream. I can see his stricken face. Hear his pleas. His passion. His fierce resolve to destroy anyone who would hurt me or my loved ones.

He wouldn't have done that if he planned to leave me. He wouldn't care if he only wanted me to bear his child.

I glance down at the ring on my finger again. "He...asked me to marry him."

Janie's mouth hands open. She sits bolt upright in bed and momentarily forgets to keep her voice down. "He what?! Are you serious?"

It feels like I'm in a dream as I spin the ring around on my thin fingers. "Yeah. And oh, Janie, it was wonderful. He built up this whole scene, just like in the movies. He put so much thought and care into it, he remembered everything I liked, everything I'd ever told him, and then he got down on one knee and..." My voice cracks, the flood of emotions taking over at last. "He gave me this ring."

"Oh, Lara." Janie takes my hand, holding it up to admire the teardrop-shaped gem. "This is beautiful. I've never seen anything like it..." She snaps her head up and looks me straight in the eye. "You said yes, right? I mean, of course you did if you have the ring, but..." Janie drops my hand and shakes her head with a shrug. "You left him behind for this?" She gestures around the sparse hospital room. "You're my sister and I love you, but I think we both know how rare it is to find someone that truly loves you."

Her eyes flick over to Iris' crib, and I don't miss the years of grief and guilt behind them. "You're going back, right?"

I swallow the lump in my throat. After wiping my face with my sleeve, I compose myself and tell her, "I...I don't know. I honestly haven't thought about it."

That's a lie. At least partially. But I've been so preoccupied with looking after Janie and Iris that everything else had to take a backseat.

Wasn't that the story of my life? Forever putting my dreams on hold for the sake of others. With good reason, of course -- we lost our parents, Janie became a single mother, and then the blight struck and took us down with it. There hadn't been much time for dreams. Not back then.

But now...

"Do you love him?" Janie wastes no time getting to the root of the problem. She never does.

It doesn't take even a second for me to answer. I don't have to question. Don't have to consider. Because everything I know and everything in my heart has already decided. "Yes."

"Then here's what we're going to do." Her eyes light up like they did when we were kids, when she had a brand new idea she couldn't wait to tell me about. "And don't interrupt until I finish, cause I know you love to do that."

I snort and roll my eyes. She's right, but I don't have to like it. "Okay. Go on."

"You're going back to that planet, and you're going to have the best damn alien wedding of all time."

"But--" Too late. I can't stop myself.

"No buts! This is an opportunity, Lara! Don't you see that? He clearly adores you, and I want you..." She trails off. "And your child...to have the life you both deserve." She sniffs, but quickly composes herself. "And before you say anything about me, here's the deal. When my leg heals, you're going back to Aesir and you're going to have your big fat alien wedding, and I'm going to be there cheering you on."

"What?" I gasp. I didn't expect that. Could we even *do* that?

"You heard me. We're a package deal, remember? You came back for me.

Now I'm going back with you. We're in this together, or not at all."

And with that, the strong front I've worked so hard to hold up for her sake breaks. With a great, choked sob, I fall into her arms. Tears flow freely now, but they're not tears of grief or sadness. They're tears of hope. Of thankfulness. I've got the best sister in the galaxy. The most adoring mate a girl could ask for. And a miracle baby on the way.

RETURNING TO AESIRHEIM

SOREN

THREE MONTHS LATER

Three months I've been without her and each day feels longer than the last. I've had no communication, no indication that she's okay or that she will come back at all.

And with the solar storms passing through our corner of the galaxy, even my little re-routing trick can't get a signal off the planet. All I have left are my memories. That, and the soft pink ring of fabric I found under the bed after she left. I think she called it a 'scrunchie'. All I know is that it smells like her, and it's the last tether I have to what could have been.

Every Aesir knows the gravity and power of a heart-mate. Children grow up dreaming of finding a fated one. But no one tells you just how devastating it can be to lose a piece of your heart like that.

When I found her, it felt like everything finally fit into place for the first time in my life. That I wasn't running, wasn't fighting an endless war anymore. I wanted to be there for her. I wanted to build a life and settle down and watch our children grow up to be big and strong.

But right at the moment I asked her to marry me, the unthinkable happened. An accident back on Earth injured her sister, and Lara chose to return and take care of her and her niece.

I couldn't blame her. How could I? Every Aesir knows how important family and loyalty are. Especially when little ones are involved.

But what about *our* little one? The thought sours in the back of my throat. *Would I ever see my child? Would I ever see either of them again?*

In the meantime, all I could do was wait. Watch. And try to pour myself into anything and everything that would take my mind off the pain.

It wasn't all bad. I threw myself into my work and my training. My muscles burned with exhaustion daily and I'd gained more than a few new scars, but it was nothing compared to the pain of missing Lara.

She's still there, a faint presence deep in my chest. I feel her when I wake and when I go to bed. I never got the chance to tell her just how much she means to me. To *show* her, the way only an Aesir can.

And I don't just mean sex. I mean the ceremonial mate-bond, the one we were supposed to share before circumstances tore us apart. As fully-bonded heart-mates, we would be able to share thoughts and feelings with one another. She would never be alone again.

I frown and clench my fists at my side. That's if, of course, she ever comes back.

Every day it seems less likely, but the distant presence of Lara's spirit stays with me. A constant reminder of what could have been.

It's no wonder some men go mad after losing a heart-mate. If I didn't have a job to do, people to serve, I would have lost it long ago.

My men give me sympathetic looks when we meet up for drinks, but none of them dare broach the topic. We shoot the shit and try to keep our spirits up as best we can, but things just aren't the same. No amount of fighting or feasting will change that.

One of my buddies had the nerve to suggest I 'take the edge off' and go to one of the Aesir whore houses. He ended up with a broken nose for that one. I don't want any random Aesir whore. I want Lara. She's the only one for me, and now that I know she's out there, I won't rest until she's in my arms again.

I find myself passing by the port more than I should. Checking the monitors, just in case. It's foolish — I know that. Especially with the storm season the way it is. But every time I pass the monitors, I envision the ticker changing and announcing a new shuttle from Earth coming in for a landing…

The sound of the port's great airlock hissing open catches my attention from across the harbor and I break into a sprint. My first thought is intruders — for who else but the sand pirates would try and make the journey in this weather? But as I grow closer my senses fill with something very different.

And very familiar.

Roses and honey, all wrapped up in the most sensuous, feminine aura I've ever smelled in my life. I'll never forget that scent as long as I live.

It's her.

By all the stars and planets, it's her!

It's the strangest sense of deja vu as I push myself faster. The sleek dome of the transport ship glides into view and begins the docking protocol. Sure enough, the monitor spells out the words I've been dying to see for the last three months:

Incoming transport from planet: Earth. Please stand back.

The hull is splattered with dust and mud, but I barely register it. It's nearing the end of the stormy season, but it's still not safe for travel out there. How this little ship made it through unscathed astounds me.

If something had happened to her…

I put on another burst of speed and I'm on the elevated metal walkways surrounding the hangar bay. The ship's still powering down, and already I can feel her presence. Her scent. Her spirit.

I'm scanning the unfamiliar architecture of the shuttle, trying to find out where she'll come out. I'm about to leap in there and rip the door open myself to get to her, so strong is the feral urge rising within me.

This is worse than the first time I saw her. It's the same possessive call to mate, to devour, but this time there's more to it. It's not just a raw primal need to reproduce — we've already done that — but my heart's on the line as well.

My mate. My Lara. Three months of empty days and emptier nights. I can't wait another second. I need her in my arms. Now.

Luckily for the ship, the gate opens and connects to the gangway before I start tearing things apart. The door opens…

And there she is, round with child, face flushed, looking around the spaceport with the same awe I fell in love with at first sight.

I throw myself over the walkway and land hard. The floor shakes and the railings rattle, but my eyes are trained on only one thing.

And at the sound of the commotion I've made, she sees me too. With a cry that sears itself into my heart, she starts running too, and I'm lost in her arms.

Her soft, warm body collides with mine and all of the pain and guilt and grief dissipates, just like that. She's here. She's mine. I bury my face in her neck and draw in a long breath, again and again. I kiss her neck, her ears, her cheeks, her forehead. She's giggling, breathless, and flushed an even deeper shade of red from my advances. I can't help myself, I'm just so happy to see her.

"Soren!" She manages to get out between kisses. "Yes, yes, I'm all right!"

My hand goes to her belly, round with my child. She's positively glowing, and I think my heart might burst at the sight. Visions of her with my young in her arms, pregnant again while our children run and play in the vast fields of Aesir fill my mind. This time, I'm not letting her leave.

HOMECOMING

LARA

Soren's hands and lips are everywhere the moment I step out of the shuttle. It's like he's trying to make up for lost time, but I can't say I'm complaining.

The entire trip back to Aesir I wrung my hands and tried not to think about the impending reunion. A small, sick part of me wondered if he'd forgotten about me. If he'd run off with some alien girl and moved on.

So many nights I laid awake wondering if he thought about me half as much as I thought about him. And now that I was here in his arms once more, I had no doubt about that.

My heart flip-flops with joy in my chest, thundering so loudly I can barely hear anything else. The universe narrows in that instant to just the two of us. To his huge, muscular body embracing mine, slotting us together like two perfect puzzle pieces. We were made for each other, he'd told me.

Destined in the stars.

There were a few nights back on Earth when I woke to a strange fluttering in my chest. I could have sworn I heard his voice. But every time, I was back in my bedroom on Earth, Janie and Iris sleeping peacefully next to me.

This time, I feel the fluttering again, and I finally realize what it was. It was him checking up on me all along. The feeling rises from my heart and spreads down my spine, tingling through my arms and legs. It's him. It's always been him.

I didn't understand what he meant about heart-mates at the time, but now I think I do.

It's because he's there with me. Even when I'm on another planet. I felt him. He watched over me. And I know that no matter what happens from here on out, I'll never be alone again.

"Soren!" I giggle, pushing him away long enough to take a breath. "I'm all right! I'm fine!"

He draws back and takes me in all over again, his eyes glistening. "I'm just so glad to see you again. I thought…" Soren doesn't finish his sentence. He drops to his knees and lays his head against my rounded belly. His big hand can nearly cover my entire stomach, even swollen as it is. But with his arms around me, I feel safer than I have in years.

"Hey there, little one," Soren mutters, rubbing the taut skin with reverence belying his size. "Daddy's here. Right here. I can't wait to see you."

I'm about to get choked up all over again. Hearing him call himself

Daddy. The softness of his words. The intensity and pure awe that he showers upon us both. I slip my fingers under his chin and tilt it upward so that he's facing me. I want to make sure he's paying attention for this part.

I look into those beautiful dark eyes and say the words that have been stuck in my heart for the last three months:

"And Soren? My answer is yes. I would love nothing more than to be your bride."

His face absolutely crumbles in shock and happiness. Soren springs to his feet and lets out a whoop, hoisting me into his arms before I even see him moving. He's peppering my forehead with kisses again, all the way down to my neck, my shoulders, my breasts…

“Wait!” I sputter amidst the rising heat between us. “Soren — ahh! Put me down!”

His eyes clear immediately and he sets me gently back on the ground. “What’s wrong? Did I hurt you? Did I hurt the baby? I’m sorry, I was just so excited, and…”

“No, it’s nothing like that!” I assure him, taking his hands in my own. There’s still one more thing I need to do. The final piece of the puzzle. I point toward the shuttle doors, and his eyes widen.

Janie, slow but moving, hobbles out of the ship with Iris on her hip. Her leg’s been fitted with a high-tech support cast, but she's still not one hundred percent. If I had it my way, she would have waited until she was fully healed, but she insisted we leave the planet at once.

I'll never tell, but I couldn't wait another second to see my Soren either.

As the Aesir sun catches the braid hanging over her shoulder, I realize just how much she looks like me.

Her face is just as awe-stricken as mine was the first time I arrived on Aesir, and sweet little Iris is awake and pawing at the air, shrieking with excitement.

My family. Together, here at last.

My heart swells so strongly I think it might burst, and in response, a subtle fluttering in my stomach awakens as well.

"Soren, I would like you to meet my sister, Janie. And my niece, Iris."

When Janie arrives at my side, she cranes her neck upward to meet Soren's gaze. I forgot, she's even shorter than I am. Soren is practically a giant next to her. Janie sticks out her free hand for a shake, but the golden warlord ignores it. Instead, he goes to one knee, fist pressed against his chest.

"It is an honor to meet you, Janie and Iris of Earth." He bows his head. "You will receive the utmost hospitality and respect here on Aesirheim, and no harm shall come to you. I swear it on the bones of my ancestors, as the stars glitter in the sky."

Even I'm moved by the formal display. Janie gapes, looking to me and then back to him. Oh, right. She doesn't have a translator yet, even though we already had to do paperwork and some medical inspections in order to get Janie and Iris to Aesirheim.

"He's welcoming you," I tell her. But it's so much more than that. "He says it's an honor to meet you and that you'll receive only the best here on Aesir."

"Oh!" Janie glows. She shoots me a knowing look. "You said he was a gentleman, but I didn't expect..."

I simply grin. "Nothing like the men back on Earth, huh?"

She snorts. "Don't get me started."

After Soren straightens, I look up at him. "I have one condition, you know. For marrying you."

"And what's that?" He raises an amused eyebrow, as if he already knows what I'm going to say.

"When I left Aesir to take care of my sister, it was one of the hardest decisions I ever had to make. I never want to have to choose between you and her ever again. So if we're going to make this work, she's staying here. With us. Her and Iris both."

"But of course!" Soren claps his hands together. "I wouldn't have it any other way. My people — my family — will be honored to greet you." He squeezes my hand. "To greet you both." He extends a hand to Janie. "And to you,

Janie of Earth, I am blessed to receive a new sister."

Janie takes his hand, intending to shake it, but Soren takes her small palm and presses a kiss to it instead. Her ears turn red first, then the rest of her face. Iris babbles and reaches out to him, her stubby fingers grasping at air.

Soren has to extend only a single finger, and she grabs onto it like it's her new favorite toy. He lets out a hearty laugh, and I can't help but do the same.

It's a laugh of relief. Of excitement. Of gratitude. And most of all, of hope.

My belly flutters again. In the span of a few short months, my own child will be here. Resting on my hip, cooing, grabbing at Soren's huge paws with their own little hands.

I can't wait.

"Come on," he tells me. Wrapping a possessive arm around my waist and bringing me close, he presses one more kiss to my waiting lips. It's warm and sweet and full of promises for the years to come. "Let's get you home."

"To the cottage?" I ask.

Soren shakes his head. "No. Not this time." He starts to call out to a dock worker, giving instructions so fast I can't keep up. "This time, you will join me at my home. With my people. Because Lara?"

"Yes?"

"It is your home now, too."

REUNITED

SOREN

At last, my heart-mate is home. Truly home.

I never thought it was possible to feel this sense of peace. Not in all my years did I expect it. Us Aesir are built and bred for war. For battle. But something about this human makes me soft in all the best ways. She brings out the protector in me. The doting, loving father and uncle.

Of course, she makes me *hard* in all the best ways, too.

Speaking of which…

We've got to make up for lost time.

Lara's sitting there, cross-legged on the couch, pointing at her tablet with Janie next to her. They're watching something, a movie it looks like. Even Iris is there, eyes wide and enraptured as the screen swirls and changes. It warms my heart to see how well they get along — I knew she was someone special when Lara chose to go back for her. Now that she's here, she's become just as much part of the family as Lara is.

My people welcomed them with open arms. Especially once they saw how happy I was around Lara. My men snickered and joked a bit behind closed doors when we were all a few drinks in, but they were some of my biggest supporters. In fact, it wasn't twenty-four hours after meeting Lara and Janie that they were asking how they could sign up for one of those Earth girls.

I chuckle and shake my head. I got lucky, I tell them. Really, really lucky. Who would have thought that I would find my heart-mate on a whole different planet?

The ending music of the movie swells and Janie takes Iris back into her arms. She gets up off the couch and stretches, giving me a little wave before heading back to the bedroom I had prepared for her.

She may not be my heart-mate, but she's my heart-mate's sister, and that's as good as. Janie and her little one deserve just as much care and devotion as my Lara. It's only proper and befitting of an Aesir warlord, after all. Women — especially mates — are to be cherished and protected at all costs. It breaks my heart to think of anyone daring otherwise.

After Janie and Iris go back to their room, I join Lara on the couch and wrap my arms around her, pulling her into a kiss. She drops the tablet onto the table, all but forgotten, and returns it in kind, her small hands pressing against my broad chest. My cock swells in anticipation; my heart thunders out a steady beat. "What do you think?" I ask before nipping at her earlobe, her neck, her shoulder. "What do you think of your new home?"

Lara lets out a sigh, tilting her head to the side to give me even more access. I take her up on it, kissing and tasting every inch of skin I can get to. She'll have a mark there come morning, but that's the point. No one will ever doubt who she belongs to when she bears my mark. They won't even try.

"It's…" Lara sighs between kisses. "It's wonderful. It's more than I could have imagined…" I swoop her up into my arms and hold her even closer, relishing the soft warmth of her skin. I missed this so much. "And you've been so kind to Janie, too. I can't thank you enough…"

"I can think of a perfect way for you to thank me." I rumble out the words and I feel her stiffen beneath me. Feel her scent heighten, her thighs clench. Her hormones practically pour off of her, surrounding me and making me dizzy.

"Oh, Soren," Lara says, burying her face into my chest. "I need you…I need this…"

"I'm here, love. I'm here." I cradle her like the treasure she is and head for the bedroom. It's time to show her just how much I missed her. How empty I was without her.

I kick the door shut behind us as I lay her down on the bed. She looks so beautiful like that, sprawled out with her hair surrounding her head like a halo. Her full lips part only slightly, her eyes lidded with desire.

I can't believe she's mine.

"Soren," Lara pants, her thighs clenching together. It doesn't matter — I can smell her arousal plain as day, and soon our sheets will be covered in it. She watches me undress with great interest, and then I go to her, slowly slipping her out of her clothes. As much as I would like to rip the fabric to shreds, I have to be gentle. She's carrying our child, and that's more important than all the rough sex in the world.

That doesn't mean we still can't have a little fun, though...

I can't believe how stunning she looks, laying there naked with her round, pregnant belly sloping away from the mattress. Fuck. My cock throbs again, hardening further and pressing up against my stomach. My balls tighten, every sense short-circuiting to focus on her and only her.

Have I always been this horny for her, or is it just the excitement of the reunion that has me feeling like this?

Either way, I'm not complaining. She sets off every alpha instinct I have, and I'm going to claim her as thoroughly and in as many ways as possible tonight.

"I missed you," Lara sighs as I run my hands down her bare skin. I want to caress every inch, memorize each plane and curve so I'm never without her again. "The hormones from the baby, I've been so pent up." A dark blush colors her already flushed cheeks as she throws her head back into the pillows. "I tried, but with my belly in the way, I can't quite reach, my fingers aren't good enough…"

"Don't worry, love. I'm here. I've got you." I knead each breast in my hand, brushing the pads of my fingers over the nipples before leaning forward to take them into my mouth. She moans and squeaks, arching her back delightfully while her arms grab on to me for dear life.

"Yes…" She pants as I suckle her nipples.

"More," Lara sighs when I move lower to worship her belly.

"Please." And her voice is practically a beg by the time I reach her mound, two fingers brushing ever so softly between her folds to find the wetness there. She's soaking wet, already starting to seep into the sheets, but I don't care. I want her messy and exhausted and fucked out, all because of me.

"This what you wanted?" I mutter as I press one finger into her, then two. Her breath hitches as she throws her head backward with a gasp.

"Yes!" The word comes out ragged and desperate.

"How about this?" I ponder, and move down to take her nub between my lips. Lara cries out, the sweetest song I've ever heard, and thrusts her hips up into my face.

"Yes…God, yes!" She wails. I use my tongue to drive her higher while pumping in and out of her wet cunt with my fingers. She's bucking and grinding against me, her hands tangled in my hair and pulling me closer, egging me on for more, more, more…

And when she shatters, it's the the most perfect thing in the world, a litany of pure adoration as she cries out my name again and again.

"I love you," I growl into her wet heat. "I love you, I love you, I love you."

She looks up at me, eyes teary and far away. A smile creeps over her blissed-out face as I pull away from her cunt. "I love you too, Soren."

And now it's time to show her just how much. Taking my cock in hand, I brush it against her seeping folds. She moans and writhes against my touch, and it drives a certain sort of pride seeing her come undone like this. My heart-mate, my Lara, reduced to nothing more than a whimpering mess under me.

No one else could do this for her. No one else knows her body as well as I do.

And as I enter her sweet heat for the first time in what feels like eternity, I know that she's made for me. We both cry out at the same time and I lean forward, boxing her in with my huge arms on either side of her small body. Fuck, she's tight.

"Oh, Lara..." I let out a deep, satisfied sigh as her walls clench around mine. I can't help teasing her a little bit when I pull out a few inches to delve into her again.

"I've missed you." A sweet, throaty moan escapes her lips.

"Missed you too, my heart-mate." I push into her even deeper. Her soft human nails dig into my back and her legs wrap around my waist. She's mine. All mine.

"But I'm here now," I promise her with another powerful thrust. Leaning forward, I nuzzle my nose against hers before giving her a kiss on her lips, her chin, her neck.

"And I'm here now." Her words so sweetly echo my own, and I want to remember this moment forever. The warm swell of her belly against me. The breathy moans. The way she arches her back just right, angling her hips up to take me deeper.

"Tell me you'll never leave me again." I say between thrusts. I know she won't, but that fierce, possessive alpha-ness roars up inside me. I need to hear her say it. I need to know she's mine, now and forever.

“Never,” she promises. I bottom out inside of her with a cry. I won’t last much longer if she keeps saying things like that. “You’re stuck with me. Forever.”

Music to my ears. I piston into her like a man possessed, my fingers digging into the soft flesh of her hips as I drive home again and again. My grunts grow louder, her soft sighs turn to wanton moans, and with a final, savage thrust, I hold her close and fill her to the brim with my seed.

We're panting, sticky messes by the end of it, but I don't care. And neither does she. We have one another once more, and I am never letting her go again.

EPILOGUE

SOREN

SOME TIME LATER

Laughter fills the air as I push open the door to my home. It's been a long day of training, but there's something sweeter about it nowadays. Knowing I have someone at home waiting for me makes it all the more special.

"Da!" A little voice cries out.

I throw my weapons and gear to the side and kick the door shut with my foot. Such carelessness would have my father rolling in his grave, but he's not here right now, is he? How can I not forget everything when my young son calls out to me so sweetly?

I go to him and his mother, kissing her on the forehead before taking the infant into my arms. He's so small, so soft…and I still can't believe it…he's mine.

Lara's pregnancy went off without a hitch, and she delivered a darling baby boy on the night of the full moon. The doctor said it was a good omen — that he would grow up to be big and strong like his father.

When I look into his little face, I see Lara's eyes looking back at me. He's a perfect combination of the two of us. Pale golden skin, Lara's eyes, and soft, chubby limbs that greedily reach out for everything. He's everything I could have asked for. He's perfect.

"How was training?" Lara asks, eyeing the bandage on my knee. "Are you hurt?"

"No, no. I'm fine." It's just a scratch, really, but she always acts like it's the end of the world. It's because she cares about me. Kind of cute, really. And when she treats my wounds so gently and so lovingly…I can't really complain.

Lara crosses her arms. She's not buying it. "Uh huh."

“I mean it!” I insist, a smile on my face.

“All right, all right.” She laughs. “Don’t get too attached — I was about to take him back to bed, poor thing’s exhausted. You know how cranky he gets when he doesn’t sleep.”

“Do I ever.” I agree. Having a newborn was the biggest blessing I could have asked for, but taking care of a child was a full time job. More than a full time job. “You’re lucky you’re so cute,” I coo at him before handing him back to his mother.

“I’ll meet you in the bathroom,” Lara says as she walks away. “I want to take a look at that wound before you get too comfortable.”

I playfully roll my eyes. “Yes, dear.”

But I don't go to the bathroom. I wait for her right outside the bedroom door, and when she comes out, I surprise her by pushing her up against the wall, letting her feel the hardness between my thighs. "Could I do this if I was injured?" I tease, dipping my head to draw in a breath at her neck. She always smells incredible, but there's a sharp tinge to it today that means only one thing: her heat is coming.

Lara gasps, her mouth open in a perfect 'o' as she looks up at me. I love pinning her like this. Love seeing her squirm beneath my touch. And, of course, she loves it too. Her scent is a dead giveaway before she even opens her mouth. "Soren…"

"Yes?" I say, a mocking grin crawling up my face. "Something the matter?"

"You..." She sputters and trips over the words. "Now?"

"Why not?" I tilt my head until my hot breath is right next to her ear. She shivers. "Why don't I prove to you just how healthy I am. Put another baby in you, just for good measure. Your heat's coming soon, isn't it?"

"Soren!" Her voice raises an octave this time. I'll never get tired of hearing it.

"That's my name, love."

"Don't you know what day it is?" Lara squirms against me, pinned between my body and the wall. I have her right where I want her.

Her question gives me pause, though. What day was it? Was I missing something?

"You'll have to tell me," I admit finally before pulling away. "I got caught up with training earlier, forgive me."

"It's all right." Her eyes shine with that kind of special happiness I've only heard about in stories. I still can't believe I've gotten so lucky. I have a heart-mate to call my very own, and we have a beautiful baby boy to love and cherish for the rest of our lives. "It's our son's naming ceremony today."

Of course. How could I have forgotten?

I take her into my arms and thank the stars all over again for bringing her to me. She pulls me into a deep kiss, and when we part I swear I can see the stars reflected in her eyes.

"Lara…" I start. There's so much emotion. I don't even know where to begin.

"Yes?"

Words will never be enough to show her how I feel. So I rest my forehead against hers, twine our fingers together, and kiss her one more time. "Thank you. For being mine."

www.ingramcontent.com/pod-product-compliance
Lightning Source LLC
Chambersburg PA
CBHW030341310726
48979CB00001B/128

* 9 7 8 1 6 3 4 8 1 0 7 3 9 *